"I should have you arrested," BJ told Flynn

"Before you call in the feds," he said around a mouthful, "I have an idea that might help us both. In fact, I've been thinking about this for a while. We both have something the other needs. What if we barter?" He moved his sandwich her way. "I do something for you— you do something for me."

She yawned. "And what do you think you can do for me? Read the rest of my mail? Sack my refrigerator again?"

"I have a better idea."

"I'm breathless with anticipation. Whatever can it be?"

"Barbara Jean Fairmont, I'm going to marry you."

Hi, Romance Lovers,

Ever wonder who that superjock in high school ended up marrying, or who that brainiac in all those advanced classes hooked up with?

A Fabulous Husband is that story. Football star, now army colonel Flynn MacIntire and studious Barbara Jean Fairmont, now the town doctor, are headed for the altar in a marriage of convenience...except nothing is convenient at all. Keeping the marriage quiet leads to more problems when friends and family find out and are doubly upset because they weren't invited.

A Fabulous Husband is the second book in my FORTY & FABULOUS series. There's nothing more fun than being in love, and being forty and in love makes this the best time of all.

Enjoy another visit to Whistlers Bend, Montana, where fun, sass and a whole lot of romance are the order of the day, and see what Maggie, BJ and Dixie are up to now.

Have fun, and visit me at DianneCastell.com and let me know what's going on in your FORTY & FABULOUS life.

Dianne Castell

P.S. I'd love to hear from you. Visit me at www.DianneCastell.com or write me at DianneCastell@hotmail.com.

— Forty & Fabulous —

A Fabulous Husband

DIANNE CASTELL

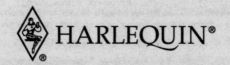

HARLEQUIN®

TORONTO • NEW YORK • LONDON
AMSTERDAM • PARIS • SYDNEY • HAMBURG
STOCKHOLM • ATHENS • TOKYO • MILAN • MADRID
PRAGUE • WARSAW • BUDAPEST • AUCKLAND

ISBN 0-373-75092-7

A FABULOUS HUSBAND

This edition published by arrangement with Harlequin Books S.A.

® and TM are trademarks of the publisher. Trademarks indicated with ® are registered in the United States Patent and Trademark Office, the Canadian Trade Marks Office and in other countries.

www.eHarlequin.com

Printed in U.S.A.

To Ann Marie...artist, adventurer and daughter
extraordinaire. Thanks for all the good times!

Dianne Castell's *The Wedding Rescue*
(February 2004) was voted
best Harlequin American Romance
of 2004 by *Romantic Times* magazine.

Books by Dianne Castell

HARLEQUIN AMERICAN ROMANCE

888—COURT-APPOINTED MARRIAGE
968—HIGH-TIDE BRIDE
1007—THE WEDDING RESCUE
1047—A COWBOY AND A KISS
1077—A FABULOUS WIFE*

*Forty & Fabulous

Chapter One

Dr. Barbara Jean Fairmont stood in the doorway of the Cut Loose Saloon and peered through the thick haze of smoke at Colonel Flynn MacIntire, the guy she'd dated for one whole month in high school until she'd told him that dressing in weird clothes and running up and down a field after an elliptical ball every Friday night was just plain stupid, and he'd told her that debating questions that had no answers was a whole lot worse.

BJ and Flynn—the Brain and the Brawn, then and always. And even after all those years, the one guy she'd never really gotten over. Was that pathetic or what!

Oh, they'd changed—she was now the revered town doctor and Flynn a true American hero—but they still had nothing in common. Why would he make the army his life's work? Never staying in one place, never having the same friends, never knowing where you'd be shipped off to next. The life from hell!

Currently, Flynn was in a different kind of hell. He was home on leave with an injured leg, and his grandmother had asked BJ to help him. And she would. Not just because Grandma Mac had made the request or because BJ was a doctor and that was what doctors did, but because *she had to get rid of him.*

Usually, her lingering and irrational attraction to him wasn't a problem because he wasn't around for her to obsess over. But now he was here, and likely to stay unless he got better and went back to the army, where he belonged, leaving her in peace in Whistlers Bend, Montana, where she belonged.

Some country-western singer warbled from the jukebox as BJ snaked her way among the well-occupied chairs. Flynn sat alone, cigarette in hand, table littered with longnecks, not doing himself one bit of good. How could he abuse his body like this? And such a fine body it was. All army, all muscle, all man. But ogling him was not why she was here. "If you quit swilling beer and puffing cancer sticks, agree to get off your butt and do therapy, maybe I can help you."

He glanced up and she gave his two-day-odd beard, wrinkled clothes and ruggedly handsome face a quick once-over and shuddered. Gads, she was more pathetic than she'd thought.

"If this is one of those tests for the inebriated, I'll flunk. So you can save your breath and go away, Fairmont."

She let out a sigh and sat down across from him. "Oh, if only I could," she said, as much to herself as Flynn.

He turned the beer bottle in circles on the scarred wood tabletop. "How'd I get to be your latest project? Doesn't anyone else in town need your expert medical care and counseling?"

"Probably, but none of *their* grandmothers pounded on my door at 6:00 a.m. clenching rosary beads in one hand and a fistful of medical records in the other."

Flynn's jaw dropped a fraction and his gaze met BJ's. "*My* medical records? They were in my duffel."

"She's a grandmother. Grandmothers interfere. It's their duty. She loves you and she's worried about you." BJ slid a folder across the table. "You never came to me with any ailments even when you were on leave, so I'm sure you didn't intend for me to be your primary-care physician now."

She tapped the folder. "Look, I considered going into orthopedics. Spent time observing treatments and therapy, and I have doctors I can confer with, if you cooperate." *Oh, please cooperate!* He was still so appealing, so not the kind of man she could ever have a relationship with. What would they talk about? What would they do? Kissing would be a good start. No kissing!

"Sounds like Grandma Mac's been tuning in to Dr. Phil and hearing about that intervention stuff again."

"Or she's concerned. Either way, she did ask me for advice and she's having me over for corned beef and cabbage in—" BJ checked her watch "—one hour and thirteen minutes."

Flynn nudged the top of the cane hanging from the table, the hooked part rocking as he studied it. His eyes clouded for a second, as his thoughts went someplace other than the saloon. "Help someone else. The good folks at Walter Reed say this thing could be a permanent fixture in my life." His eyes met hers for a moment. "And why doesn't she fix corned beef and cabbage for me?"

"She doesn't think you're trying hard enough to get better and you shouldn't have left the hospital before they discharged you, and no one wants to upset the town hero by suggesting he's screwing up his life."

"Except you? The Brain and the Brawn just like old times." He took another swig of beer and a drag off his cigarette, watching the smoke fade into the air. "So, you're here because of a bribe of corned beef and cabbage."

He leaned back and folded his arms across his solid, broad chest. The index finger on his left hand was slightly crooked, as if it had been broken and not set properly; he had a thin scar on his neck, a wider, newer one at his chin and he was graying at the temples. A soldier. A *fighting* soldier, who'd seen more than his share of combat. She could only imagine what he'd been through and she hated it. But he'd returned alive, and that was something to be hugely thankful for.

"You haven't changed since high school, BJ Fairmont. You think you know all the answers."

"No, that would be you," she said, her doctor attitude rising to the occasion, shoving everything else—even her latent Flynn desires—out of the way, because getting him better was what really mattered. "Right now I'm your last hope, MacIntire." She stood and leaned over the table, meeting his gaze. "I'm all that stands between Flynn MacIntire, army man, and Flynn MacIntire, civilian. If your leg doesn't improve, the *Colonel* part of your name is history, or you get to shuffle papers in some local recruiting office till you retire. I have an obligation as a doctor to help you, and I will if you let me. Until then, I'll save you leftovers. See you around, Colonel."

"Anyone ever tell you you're a pain in the ass?"

"All the time. I've got it on the little plaque right below my medical degree," she told him, and headed out.

She pushed the door open and stepped onto the sidewalk, blinking to acclimate from dark interior to bright July sunlight as she mumbled, "Well, gee, that went well."

"Talking to yourself isn't so bad." Dixie's voice, coming from behind, put BJ in a much better mood. "It's when you start answering that you got to worry."

BJ turned and smiled at the second member of the Fearsome Threesome, as everyone in town had called her, Dixie and Maggie for the past twenty-five years. "Nice blouse. Any chance you bought one for me in blue?"

Dixie sashayed in a little circle, twitching her hips and showing off her new clothes. Nobody sashayed like Dixie Carmichael. Nobody did *anything* like Dixie. She hooked her arm through BJ's and continued down the street, saying, "Pretty and Pink's having a sale. You better get your fanny over before all the good stuff's gone. Maggie's there now, picking the place clean for her honeymoon."

Dixie nudged BJ. "Any reason I should go back and buy *baby* things for you?"

BJ's heart tightened. "I don't think so. The letter from the adoption agency is less than encouraging. Being single, having a demanding job and turning the big 4–0 last week didn't put my name on top of their adoption pile."

"I still think you should try the old-fashioned method. Be good for you."

"I did that, remember? Nearly married Randall Cramer. Believed I was in love with him. But I was really in love with the idea of having a family. And besides, all the wanting in the world won't compensate for low progesterone levels."

She squeezed BJ's arm a little tighter. "We'll figure something out. The three of us always do. There are a lot of alternatives these days. Right now, though, let's grab a bite at the Purple Sage before my shift starts, and you can tell me what you were doing in the saloon. Picking up some vices, I hope."

"Does Flynn MacIntire count as a vice?" BJ pulled open the door to the diner, inhaling the smells of America—cheeseburgers, hot fries, coffee and apple pie. 'Course, it would be much healthier for everyone in Whistlers Bend if the cheese didn't have the burger, the potatoes were boiled, the coffee decaf and the apple not pied.

Dixie's eyes twinkled. "Flynn MacIntire always counts, and if vice is involved so much the better." They slid onto chairs at their usual table by the window. She continued. "And *you* talked to *him*? What in the world brought that on? You two never talk—least, haven't since high school. Remember when he pulled your panties up the high-school flagpole, read your diary over the loudspeaker and called you brainiac?"

"And I put oatmeal in his football helmet and wrote

articles about jocks running up and down the football field because they couldn't find their way out?"

"You two breaking up had to be one of the ten best breakups of all time, though in my opinion it was a cover-up, that you still liked each other and just didn't know how to make the relationship work."

"Trust me, that is one relationship that would never ever work."

"Darn shame, if you ask me. But word has it the *hunky* one—"

"The *hunky* one?" BJ rolled her eyes. "Where'd that come from?"

"From every woman in town except you." Dixie's expression turned salutary. "Flynn's the king of hunky. Anyway, he's got six weeks to report back to his base in acceptable physical condition—though his delicious physical condition's always looked real acceptable to me."

Ditto, BJ thought. When Flynn was around she couldn't concentrate without him jumping into her brain, and she couldn't sleep without Flynn being right in the middle of it. "Grandma Mac asked me to help with his leg and I told Flynn I might be able to if he'd give me a chance and start taking care of himself. You can guess how well that went over."

Dixie pursed her lips. "You really believe an army guy like Flynn is going to accept advice from a tall skinny blonde in Gucci loafers and Armani slacks? The only coordinated thing about you is your wardrobe. Like Schwarzenegger following bodybuilding advice from Bill Gates. You're a wimp—Flynn's Rambo. Why should he listen to you?"

BJ held out her hands and gave her the *duh* look. "Because I'm a doctor? What do I have to do—wear camouflage?"

"You'd look really bad in camouflage. Now, me…I look great in greens and browns with my red hair."

They ordered tea, Dixie adding a slice of chocolate cake. She propped an elbow on the table and rested her chin in her hand. "Don't you think if there was an easy answer to helping Flynn he would have gotten better in the hospital?"

"He's given up, Dix. He's not trying anymore. I can see it in his eyes and so can Grandma Mac. One day Flynn just walked out of Walter Reed, bought a car and drove straight through to Whistlers Bend."

Dixie sighed. "Breaks the heart, doesn't it."

"Sympathy isn't what MacIntire needs. He needs…" BJ grinned, feeling a brainstorm coming on. "Something else." BJ leaned close to avoid the gossips. "What if he suddenly wanted, *really* wanted, to get better?"

She flashed a wicked smile. "What if Rambo got outdone by the tall skinny girl who couldn't bounce a ball and chew gum at the same time?"

"Sounds like a throwback to high school, and that was a long, long, long time ago."

"Not that long ago. When I was talking to Flynn over at the Cut Loose he mentioned it—the Brain and the Brawn. All I have to do is do the things he can't do now. I'll show him up and he'll hate that."

The food arrived, and Dixie forked a chunk of cake and wagged it at BJ. *"That's it?* That's your great idea?

Don't you ever watch James Bond? Now, *that* man has great ideas."

BJ stole a bit of cake, plopped it in her mouth and said around a mouthful, "That's the only idea I've got, Dixie. Someone's has to kick Flynn in the ass."

"Don't kick too hard. That man has such a fine ass." Dixie gave BJ an evil look as she went for more cake. "You could just order a piece, you know."

"Can't. I'm the one peddling fruits and veggies around here, remember? Besides, your cholesterol is too high already. I'm saving you."

"Bite me." Dixie licked icing from the fork. "If you're messing with Flynn sex should be involved."

BJ choked and Dixie said, "That's what you get for stealing my cake."

BJ gulped water. "I know Flynn's Achilles' heel, Dixie. I know what drives the man bonkers." She pointed to her chest and grinned. "Me, and that definitely rules out sex. The Brain is going to beat the Brawn at his own game and get him back in the army, where he belongs." *And out of my life so it can get back to normal!*

TWO HOURS LATER as BJ pulled on a pair of running shoes, she felt sure her great plan would work just fine. *It had to.* After an hour of Grandma Mac and her scrapbook of Flynn the football star, Flynn at Virginia Military Institute, Flynn the war hero in Kosovo, Iraq the first time, Afghanistan, Iraq the second time. Lots and lots of pictures of Flynn in uniform and with his tanks. Couldn't he just carry a notebook and be with the press corps? Did he have to be so blasted macho, and why in the world did she like it so much? She was a geek. She should be attracted to an accountant. But she wasn't. She was more attracted to Flynn than ever.

It didn't matter, though, because soon he'd be gone, or at least improving and on his way to being gone. She slid her cell phone in her back pocket for emergency calls and stuck her hair under the Smith and Hawkins baseball cap she'd gotten for buying two new rose-bushes and a garden trowel. She caught her reflection in the full-length mirror, took off her cap and stuffed it under her T-shirt. *BJ Fairmont, five months pregnant.* She arched her back pushing the hat out farther. *BJ Fairmont, seven months pregnant.*

Except, there'd never be any months because she'd never be pregnant. Forty was too high-risk for a first pregnancy and not much better for adoption. Why hadn't she started on this sooner? Because somewhere deep inside, she thought she'd marry. Even after Randall Cramer had left her standing at the altar ten years ago with the entire town in attendance, she'd still thought she'd find her man, someone to love and to love her in return. And then suddenly she was forty with no man and no baby.

The *man* she could do without. She had a life, a very meaningful and fulfilling one. What she really wanted was a baby. But enough of the baby blues. Right now she had to deal with Flynn MacIntire and get her sanity back, or at least have it looming on the horizon.

She went downstairs to the first floor, through her now-deserted office, which she'd decorated herself, examining rooms on one side, waiting room on the other. She locked the side door behind her, inhaled the sweet aroma of her rose garden, then crossed the street and headed for the lake. Grandma Mac had said Flynn fished there every night. It was a perfect place for BJ to implement her plan.

Evening sunlight had turned the July sky purple and pink, the Pryor Mountains in the distance amber and shades of gold. Stillness had settled over the earth—Montana caught between day and night. She spotted Flynn at the end of a dock, sitting on the edge, fishing pole in one hand, beer in the other, leaning against a piling, his back to her. She thought of senior year when he'd run track. Poetry in motion. Now he was a man. *All man.* Poetry had morphed into mature muscle, coupled with a string of heroics a mile long. Her mouth went dry. Where had that sweat above her lip come from? *She didn't sweat. Ha!*

She took off toward Flynn, ignoring the broad shoulders that tapered nicely into a trim waist. "Catch anything?" she asked when she got to him, still jogging in place, all of a sudden wishing she hadn't taken seconds of corned beef and cabbage at Grandma Mac's.

He looked up at her and rolled his eyes. "What the hell do you think you're doing…besides scaring my fish with all your stomping around? What kind of team is Smith and Hawkins?"

"I'm just out for a little exercise—running exercise. Getting all hot and sweaty." *Mostly over you.* She had to forget that. Instead, she concentrated on keeping her arms moving in time with her legs. *Left side, right side, left side, right side.*

"You? Sweat? You never sweat a day in your life."

She gave him her best indignant stare and swiped her upper lip. "See, sweat. Because I like to run, stay fit, keep in shape." She tipped her chin. "You're just too busy guzzling beer to notice." She jogged up the dock, then down.

"Yeah, you're a regular Marathon Man."

Man? Her eyebrows pulled together. "I am *not* a man." She jogged closer, trying to remember what foot went with which hand to keep up the even rhythm, suddenly feeling really winded and very tired and sick from running on a full stomach of corned beef and cabbage. Running outside was not like walking fast on her treadmill in her office. "In case you didn't notice I am not a—"

She burped, felt nauseous, grabbed for a piling to steady herself, missed and stumbled into the water. *Water!* She held her nose between her finger and thumb and used her other hand to splash her way to the surface. She spluttered.

"Stand up."

"I think I'm drowning!"

"The water's only four feet deep."

She straightened her legs and touched bottom. *"Ohthankgod!"*

She let go of her nose, pushed back her hair and looked to Flynn. He had an amused expression on his face and was dangling her hat from the end of his cane. She snagged it, wrung it out and put it on, the bill drooping over her left eye.

"Didn't you ever learn how to swim?"

"I'm terrified of water except to drink, and then I use little glasses. Heights don't do much for me, either." She shivered. "This water's really cold."

He sat on the top of a piling and tipped his head to the side, and a grin turned his lips. "I noticed. And so will anyone else who happens by."

"Noticed?" She glanced down, her nipples pressing against her wet T-shirt. How could that happen with an almost A-cup size? She folded her arms across her chest and Flynn's jacket landed over her head. Not all bad, since now he couldn't see her blush. She shrugged into the jacket, glad it fit like a small tent.

He waggled his cane at her. "Grab ahold so you don't slip and fall. The fish have had their quota of belly laughs for one day."

She didn't want his help, but she didn't want to fall again. A woman could stand just so much humiliation in one day. She grabbed on and shuffled across the rocky bottom toward the dock. Flynn held on to the piling, gripped her wrist and hauled her up onto the dock as if she were no more than a big floundering trout. "Quit wiggling."

"I'm trying to lift myself out."

"Well, don't. I've got you. You should eat more. You're as scrawny as you were in high school."

"Oh, thank you very much for the trip down memory lane." She wanted to make some smart-alecky comment to salvage what little dignity she had left, but she couldn't think of one thing. Besides, Flynn's big strong hand was around her wrist. How'd someone get that strong?

Then she remembered that one month they were together and how he used to pick her up and swing her around in his arms. Her heart beat faster and she didn't feel cold at all.

Flynn studied her. "Say something sarcastic. You always say something sarcastic. Are you okay?"

No!

She sat up and he shook his head. "I have no idea what the hell you're doing out here, but I suggest you give the plan up. You're too old to be jogging around the lake or—"

"*Old?* I'm the same age as you."

A little smile that wouldn't be contained pulled at his lips. "Men handle it better."

"Look, buster. I'm handling forty just fine."

"Yeah, you probably are. BJ Fairmont handles everything just fine."

The flat scar at his chin, pale against his unshaven face, reminded her who he was. A scar like that didn't come from some nine-to-five job behind a desk, but from protecting her and everyone else in this country.

She stood and walked down the dock, her running shoes squishing out puddles on the planks. She peered back at Flynn as he baited his hook. "I suppose I owe you a thanks, but the water was only four feet deep, so I wasn't in immediate peril."

"Except you didn't know it was four feet deep," he said without even glancing her way, the smile straining once again.

Blast the man. She made for her house. Not only had her plan failed miserably, but he'd gotten in the last word, she'd have to launder his jacket and she'd have to come up with another idea to outperform him. Running had been the easiest solution. Actually, her *only* solution.

What else could BJ Fairmont possibly do better than Flynn MacIntire? There had to be something.

THE NEXT AFTERNOON the sun dropped toward Beartooth Mountains as Flynn called it a day. He tossed his toolbox and cane into the trunk of the car, his *automatic transmission* vehicle because he couldn't drive the damn stick-shift trucks of MacIntire and Sons Construction and glanced back at the big lodge nestled against the mountainside. Kean and Scully, his brothers, and the crew were hoisting sheets of plywood on the roof of MacIntire and Sons' latest job. Flynn thought of the staircase Kean, the eldest son, had worked on today because he himself couldn't climb the ladders to the roof to help.

He massaged his leg. The doctors had said that the bullet wound to his thigh and the shrapnel damage to his knee could improve with time and exercise…*or not.* From the tone of the docs' voices the *or not* definitely had the edge. At least Flynn had an edge, not like the two soldiers, *his soldiers,* who'd died in that attack.

He'd had to leave D.C., the hospital. Remembering the attack, the men, was…hell. He could do that in Whistlers Bend, where he could get to his beer, cigarettes and fishing pole and everybody had enough sense to leave him alone—except Barbara Jean Fairmont. *What the hell was with that?*

He thought of yesterday and her falling into the lake. Her running—or whatever she was doing—where he fished couldn't be a coincidence. For years they'd avoided each other, and now all at once he'd seen her twice in one day. He hadn't seen her that many times in one day since high school.

He recalled the month they'd dated. The attraction had been there—no doubt about that. BJ was some kind of kisser. Not right off—he was probably the first boy she'd ever kissed, but once she'd gotten the hang of it… He smiled to himself. She'd really gotten the hang of it.

He recalled the oatmeal-in-the-helmet incident and the stupid jock article. He'd kept the article stashed in his duffel just for kicks, even read it a few times when he was away in one hellhole or another. He knew BJ Fairmont pretty damn good. Did she still have a passion for those marshmallow Peeps things? Still like soft pink sweaters, still flip her long blond hair back from her face when she was nervous? She still wore only a touch of makeup, which didn't cover her freckles, and only a kiss of lipstick.

Kiss? His insides stirred. Why did he have to recall so damn much?

He put the car into gear and Fairmont out of his mind, and headed for home. He should get his own place soon. Once the army kicked him to the curb, he wouldn't want to see the sympathy and disappointment on his parents' and grandmother's faces every time he came into the house with his cane. He'd never needed a place of his own before—had never been home long enough to use it. But now…he needed space.

He rounded the lake, which reflected the pine-treed mountains in the background, then turned onto the main drag—if a two-lane road could be called main—and waved to Jack Dawson in his cruiser. Whistlers Bend was damn lucky to have a veteran Chicago cop as sheriff. Flynn passed the Show and Tell, then the small cluster of spruce trees in the town square as BJ Fairmont came straight at him—*on a motorcycle?*

What the hell was Barbara Jean Fairmont doing on a damn Harley? She couldn't even ride a bicycle. The woman had nowhere near the strength to control a muscle machine like that. She was heading for disaster.

And he couldn't stop it!

He slammed on the brakes; cold sweat trickled down his chest as he watched tragedy unfold before his eyes. She wasn't going that fast, which gave him time to swerve left to avoid her. He could see that her green eyes were round in confusion. She was going to crash, be injured or worse. She veered at the last minute, bumped over the street curb, ran between concrete pots and into the pines. Her body flopped one way and the Harley dropped over on its side the other way. She lay lifeless on the ground.

Flynn stared at her, suddenly seeing two soldiers' bodies lying lifeless lying on the dusty ground…bombs exploding, fire everywhere, the smell of death filling the air. His stomach tied into a knot, bile rose in his throat, his heart raced and sweat drenched his clothes. He couldn't help them, *his men*. What damn good was he? He shook his head hard, bringing himself back to the moment, and ran toward BJ. He bent and felt for a pulse.

"Those fingers go anywhere else and you're dead meat."

Everyone who'd gathered around laughed and Flynn forced himself to breathe. *She was fine.* Everything was fine, *this time.* He gulped in air, getting himself under control. He faked a laugh, too, and swiped the sweat from his forehead, feeling the presence of Whistlers Bend surround him, instead of that of a war zone half a world away.

He turned her over and she stared at the sky. "Well, darn."

Snooky Anderson ran up, then hunkered beside BJ, his coveralls emitting the familiar fragrance of Valvoline oil mixed with transmission fluid. On Snooky it smelled just right. "Doc?" he said in a panic. "You okay? I should never have let you talk me into letting you ride the hog. What was I thinking?"

He placed her pale hand in his huge grease-smudged ones, which could fine-tune the most cantankerous carburetor and carry around a radiator as if it were a Tinker Toy.

Flynn shook his head. "Hope you have good insurance, Fairmont. That's an expensive machine you just wrecked."

"No need for insurance," Snooky said, still looking at BJ. "Last week this little lady delivered my twin boys in the back seat of my pickup in the pouring rain 'cause Trixie and I couldn't make it to Billings." His deep voice shook. "Tell me you're okay."

She patted his hand. "I'm just fine. I know you showed me how to shift, but I forgot that part, and I forgot the stopping part and all the rest of the part. Actually, I don't get it at all. Do they make Harleys in an automatic?"

Snooky gave her a wide-eyed look. "Uh, I don't think so."

She sat up and let out a sigh. "The mystique of motorcycles escapes me. Guess I won't be the poster girl for the Harley-Davidson company anytime soon."

Snooky picked her up and balanced her carefully on her feet. "Least you landed in the grass. You should have worn the helmet."

"I only intended to go to the end of your driveway, remember. The thing just ran off with me on it, and… how do you stop that thing again?"

Everyone laughed, and Snooky brushed grass from her arms and picked a stick out of her hair. "I'll show you, but you have to wear the helmet this time no matter what."

"I think I terrorized the population of Whistlers Bend enough and caused you way too much grief. My motorcycle days are over."

She grinned at the gathering crowd and opened her arms wide. "I'm fine. Evening office hours are still five to nine. Show's over. You can all leave now. And remember to thank me for supplying you with dinner gossip."

Everyone laughed again as they headed off. Snooky snatched BJ into a bear hug that made her eyes bulge and forced the air right out of her lungs in an audible *whoosh* as her feet left the ground. "Thank the Lord you're all right. Trixie would have my scalp if I let anything happen to you."

He set her down, patted her on the head, snagged a fistful of blue flowers from a decorative concrete pot and placed them in BJ's hand. "There. You take care now, Doc." He pulled up the Harley and pushed it toward Snooky's Garage.

BJ sniffed the flowers, smiled, still looking a little dazed, then started to walk away until Flynn gripped her arm. Her smooth bare skin against his hot palm made his heart skip a beat. Her unique scent mixing with the flowers she held filled his head, crowding out the war ghosts that kept him awake most nights. He held her for a second longer, some part of him not quite ready to let her or the tranquillity that she offered go, and then he remembered why he was there. "What are you doing, Fairmont? You have no business on a Harley or jogging. You and I both know that. If something happens to you, everyone's in a mess around here. There's some plan in that big brain of yours, something to make you take these chances, and what in the hell does it have to do with me?"

Chapter Two

BJ shrugged. "A lot of doctors own Harleys and jog, and why would you believe anything I do concerns you?"

Flynn didn't believe her for a military minute. "You really are a terrible liar. And you have enough sense to care for yourself for the town's sake, unless you have a good reason and that happens to be me. I don't want to be your reason, BJ."

She gave him a hard look, taking in every inch of him in one glance, sizing him up the way doctors do. "Where's your cane? Why is your shirt soaked with perspiration? It's not hot today. Are you feeling okay? Are you sick?"

He went perfectly still, remembering the flashback to the ambush. More sweat slithered down his back and he swallowed the nausea. He forced a grin and kept his eyes focused straight ahead. He was good at faking well-being. Had been doing it for months. "I forgot the cane when this lunatic on a bike came at me head-on."

His eyes locked with hers and he could see the concern there. His gut twisted. She'd been an accident waiting to happen and he couldn't stop it. *Just like the ambush, where he'd lost two good men and couldn't do a damn thing to help them.* His throat closed for a second; he couldn't breathe.

"Want to talk?" she said in a quiet voice. "I'm a good listener."

He pulled in a deep breath and got himself under control. "Yeah. Stay the hell off motorcycles and don't aim for me when you're on 'em." He aimed for his car, his leg throbbing, his shirt more drenched than before. Two men gone, two *more* men he couldn't save. How many had there been over the years. So many, way too many.

She caught up and walked beside him. "You should talk to somebody, Flynn."

He stopped and faced her. "Leave me the hell alone. Go back to doing whatever you do and forget I exist, BJ."

Her eyes hardened a fraction. "You don't have to talk to me, but you better talk to somebody. Whatever's eating you is not going away by itself. I know you. Something's wrong and it's serious."

He got back in the car, charged the engine and made for the Cut Loose, leaving BJ Fairmont in his wake. He wanted a beer. Several. A couple packs of cigarettes. Not that anything could make him forget. Those things just made him mellow. The best he could do, probably the best he could *ever* do.

THE NEXT MORNING BJ sipped coffee in her kitchen behind the office and gazed out the window as morning filled her garden. Robins, cardinals, meadowlarks, doves swooped in for breakfast at the feeders and sang as they groomed at the stone birdbath. Butterflies and moths darted about blooms in every color she could find. Two dragonflies played follow the leader over the little fountain by the sidewalk and a hummingbird feasted on the Blaze roses billowing over the back fence. A perfect morning, and the exact opposite of her motorcycle escapade yesterday. What a fiasco.

The clock in the hallway bonged seven times and her left eye twitched as the phone rang. *Mother!* Right on time. Not that talking to her mother was a bad thing. But what would it be today? An update on the social events at the country club? For sure the usual words of wisdom, like: *Barbara Jean, you really need to get out more, dear.* Or, *At forty you're not a spinster, dear, just selective, but I think it's time you selected.*

BJ knew this all came from concern for her happiness. Margaret Fairmont had loved being the town doctor's wife, doing philanthropic work and having the biggest and loveliest house, with everything perfect—including BJ. She wanted the same for her one and only child. BJ hated to disappoint her, but the perfect family was not in BJ's future.

BJ answered the phone and sorted her mail into bills and not bills as her mother talked. She reread the latest letter from Washtash International Adoption Agency and wrote a check for her phone bill as her mother started in on the country-club social agenda and the charity auction for college scholarships. BJ came across a picture of Snooky and Trixie's twins. She took care of everyone else's children in town, but she'd never get to take care of her own.

She offered a substantial donation to her mother's latest project to revamp the town square, figuring it was the least she could do since she'd put motorcycle tracks through the middle. Her mother had just launched into the current list of available men in Whistlers Bend, when BJ heard the back door open and footsteps. She spotted Maggie Moran in the hallway that separated the examining rooms.

"Mother!" BJ interrupted. "I have a patient who really doesn't look all that good. I'll call you tomorrow, I promise. We'll do lunch next week. My treat. I love you."

She disconnected just as Maggie stumbled into the kitchen. "Do you have coffee? Please tell me you have coffee—and none of that healthy decaf stuff."

"What are you doing in town so early? Guess you're not looking for your delicious, soon-to-be husband or you wouldn't be here in my kitchen looking like…this."

Maggie claimed a chair at the table. "Jack's got a sheriffs' meeting in Billings today, and I'm searching for Andy the wonder buffalo. I can't believe he's been on the loose for three weeks now. That mangy no-good animal peeked in Mrs. Gimbell's bedroom window last night and scared the poor woman to death. Can you imagine seeing this big buffalo head? Probably snorted and messed her window. Anyway, she called Roy at midnight, and being the good deputy he is, he went over and calmed her down. If you have any ideas on how to catch a runaway buffalo, I'd really like to hear them. I'm desperate here."

BJ retrieved a cup and poured coffee. She handed it to Maggie as she sat at the kitchen table. "Nice try at the small talk, but the real reason you drove to town and barged in here is to find out why I was on Snooky's Harley yesterday and what Flynn MacIntire has to do with it."

"There is that." Maggie sipped the coffee. "Heard you fell in the lake and Flynn gave you his jacket. So, how is the great Flynn MacIntire project that Dixie told me about progressing? Any signs he's weakening and going to let you help him with his leg?"

"Any signs hell's freezing over?" She pulled out a chair and sat. "Snooky's Harley has been treated and released. As for Andy, what happened for his Peeps addiction? Isn't that how you raised him to go where you wanted him to? What about leaving a trail of Peeps from town back to the ranch."

"That's about ten miles of Peeps. It doesn't matter, anyway. Seems the old boy's on a Peeps strike." Maggie leaned closer. "Right now I want to know what's next in your great plans to outdo Flynn. Come on, give. Because I know you're not throwing in the towel. You two butted heads in high school, but not all the time. I remember one very good month when you walked around on cloud nine and had a stupid grin on your face."

"That was a long time ago, and right now Flynn MacIntire wants no part of, or anything to do with, me. So, this time he wins."

"Wins as in you can't think up another idea at the moment but will soon?"

"As in the man's beyond me. My ego got in the way of my good sense. I went to Flynn, shot off my big mouth that I could help him stay in the army, but I can't." She felt sick at the confession. However, it was true, and she had no idea how to make it not true.

Maggie put down her cup. "You're a doctor. You can do this. I know you're not an orthopedic specialist, but you do all sorts of things around here. You just seem to know how, like your dad did."

"Let's just say my naive attempt to outdo him so he'd let me help fell flat on its face. Or, more accurately, *I* fell flat on *my* face. And never was a fall so justly deserved. I'm going to find him today, fess up to what I've been doing and apologize. He'll be thrilled to have me out of his hair, what little there is of it. Whatever he does, it's got to be his choice. He needs help, but not from me. I'm a small-town doctor who has no idea what war is like. He doesn't see me as anyone who can help him."

Maggie rinsed her cup in the sink. "Sure wish I could be around for that apology. Flynn might kiss you, the way he did the last time you apologized."

BJ went perfectly still, feeling the hair on the back of her neck stand up. "What *last time?*"

Maggie stacked her cup in the dishwasher and scoffed. "You know what last time I'm talking about. In high school, when you apologized for that dumb jock article after you two broke up and declared war on each other. Dixie and I were hiding in the bleachers when you cornered him after football practice. You told him you were out of line, the article was over the top and you should never have written it, and he grabbed you and kissed you, then trotted off."

She fanned herself with her hand. "It was a really good kiss, too. That's my kind of apology, though it was a darn shame he left just when things were getting interesting."

"You hid in the bleachers?"

Maggie faced her and grinned. "We're best friends. We share everything."

Not everything, BJ thought as she grabbed her cell phone from the counter. They had no idea she was still attracted to the man. She headed out the door. "I better get going. I have afternoon office hours. Flynn's helping his brothers with Sam Maxwell's new lodge up in the mountains. I can apologize there. I've given this town enough gossip to last the next year."

BJ locked the door, and Maggie said as they walked through the garden, "Call and tell me what happens."

"I can tell you that now," she said at the trellis of Blaze roses. "There'll be a lot of eating crow on my part, a lot of happiness on his, and this time there will be no kissing."

AN HOUR LATER BJ parked her SUV in front of a new post-and-beam lodge. On the drive out, she thought of Flynn's kisses a million years ago. She'd never kissed a boy before Flynn. He'd taught her, and then they'd taught each other. Shouldn't this memory have faded by now? It hadn't. She could still imagine his lips on hers. Not good. She needed to forget and get over him once and for all.

After the apology she'd steer clear of him, get involved with other men, make Mother happy. She could take part in the social gatherings for charity at the country club, as her mother wanted. Then again, it would be so much easier and less painful just to join a nunnery.

BJ gazed at the huge structure that Sam Maxwell, the Indiana Jones of Whistlers Bend, was having built. He'd worked his fanny off to make a go of Adventures Unlimited and build his incredible lodge for his customers. The lakes below and Beartooth Mountains behind made it a little piece of paradise.

She waved to Scully and Kean on the roof, the racket of their power nailers and saws fracturing the Montana peace and giving all wildlife within a ten-mile radius a migraine. The brothers stopped long enough to say their families were fine and inquire about her mother.

The steep gables that seemed to touch the sky made BJ glad she'd finally talked the senior MacIntire into retiring. Jake, with Mary, in Tahiti beat the heck out of Jake on that roof.

She picked her way over piles of lumber and around stacks of bricks and slate and walked through the opening that served as a door. "Anybody home?"

"Out for a little rock climbing or something else to bring your life to a speedy end?" Flynn said behind her.

Every day he seemed a little worse, eyes darker, mouth tight. A man alone who prided himself on having the answers and leading the way, till now. "I came to apologize."

Flynn's right eyebrow arched and he leaned against one of the rough-hewn logs holding up the second floor.

"Now, *that* one I didn't expect. You never cease to amaze me, BJ Fairmont. Apologize for what?"

"Trying to persuade you to let me help you. The truth is, I can't because your problem's in your brain."

His left eyebrow arched to meet his right. "This is probably the first time in a long time you've acknowledged I have one."

"Something's going on with you, Flynn, that I can't fix. You should get help, and—" she rushed on before he exploded "—you have to *talk* to somebody and do it soon…please."

"If this is your idea of an apology, it sucks."

"I'm getting there, but you get the lecture first because I drove all the way out here. I was trying to push your buttons. I thought if you watched me, the inept one, doing things you did so easily, you'd get royally ticked off and start working harder to get better. That was a simplistic approach to a very complex problem, and until I saw you after I wrecked the Harley I didn't realize how complex."

"Now you think I'm complex? All this flattery at one time is hard to take."

"Well, don't fall into a swoon. You're thickheaded, arrogant and have an overinflated ego, but you're hurting, and not just your leg. You could have post-traumatic stress syndrome or delayed stress syndrome. Either in any form requires attention from a professional."

"Dr. Freud, I presume?"

She'd hoped to see a flicker of acknowledgment in his blue eyes, something that hinted he agreed with her about counseling. But that didn't happen. Anger tore through her and she refused to let him off the hook. "You can smart-mouth me all you want, but you know I'm right and—"

Kean strode into the lodge, blood trickling from his wrapped hand. He zeroed in on BJ. "Howdy, Doc. Good thing you're here. We can use your satellite phone. I think Scully broke his damn leg up on the damn roof."

BJ took Kean's hand and unwound his shirt, which he'd wrapped around it. "What happened to you?"

"I reached for Scully when he fell and ran my damn hand across the damn saw. Scully will need some help getting down. Usually, we have a full crew working, but today they're trucking in supplies and having a little R & R over in Billings. We've been on the job nonstop getting this place buttoned while we still have the weather."

Flynn snagged his cane and headed outside as BJ extracted an ironed handkerchief from her back pocket and pressed it to the wound. Ironed handkerchiefs were worth their weight in gold to a doctor—a little priceless advice from Dr. Dad, God rest his soul. "You'll need stitches, but for now make a fist—not too tight—and let up every five minutes. Stay here, keep your hand elevated above your heart and rest. I'll go out and see how Scully's doing."

"I got to go with you. I'll go nuts in here." She followed Kean outside. Flynn waved to Scully and he waved back. Flynn said, "Looks like he's doing okay."

She pulled her satellite phone from her pocket and handed it to Flynn. "Tell Billings Memorial who you are and that you're calling for me. That we need airlift asap. The number's on speed dial. Give directions.

Flares to mark our location are in my car. Call the fire department. The volunteers will know how to get Scully down from a roof like this. They rescue climbers from the mountains all the time." She pointed to a pile of bricks and said to Kean, "Sit there and hold your hand cradled at your chest."

Flynn's eyes met hers, the blue more intense than a moment ago. "Where the hell are *you* going?"

She nodded to the roof. "To help Scully."

"That's probably the most insane thing I've ever heard you say, and I've heard plenty. It's a broken leg, Fairmont. The fire department will get Scully, just like you said. He'll be okay. Pissed because this will set the project back, but okay."

"Unless he passes out or goes into shock or just gets a little woozy and slides off that roof like—

"Like a greased pig down a playground slide," volunteered Kean.

"I'm a doctor. I'm going up to help your brother. This is what I do. Just make the damn calls, okay?"

She started for her car, but Flynn blocked her path. "You can't even walk down a dock without falling in the water, for Pete's sake."

"I was jogging then. I probably won't jog on the roof."

He leveled her a look that said he meant business and she'd better damn well do as he said. She imagined a lot of soldiers had seen that expression. He said, "You're inept," he told her. "Just said so yourself. And you're forty. Forty-year-old women do not climb around on roofs, *especially you.*"

"But forty-year-old men can do whatever they want, right?" she scoffed.

His jaw set in a firm line as he towered over her.

"Is that some military-authority stance meant to make soldiers do what you tell them? Well, I've got news for you, Colonel MacIntire. This isn't the military, and I'm not a soldier. I'm the doctor, this is my town, my people, and what I say goes here, so get used to it."

She walked around him, grabbed her medical bag from her SUV, and started toward the house, Flynn right behind her. "We'll argue again tomorrow, all day if you like. You can even go first." She gazed back at him. "But for now just get the fire department and helicopter here."

FLYNN CALLED HIMSELF every name for idiot. Scully was hurt and he couldn't do one damn thing to help his own brother. How could this happen? How could he let this happen? What kind of man was he?

Fairmont walked off and he was relegated to hobbling on a cane and ringing up the fire department, then the hospital. He made the calls as she climbed the ladder to the roof, her father's old black medical bag hanging from her belt, which she'd made into a sling across her chest.

"I should have gone with her," Kean said at his side.

"Not with that hand. You would have really torn it open. I should be the one up there with her."

"Well, it's a cinch somebody should. Look at her. Didn't she ever climb on monkey bars when she was little, take PE in high school?"

"I think they gave her a special dispensation."

"She's done this sort of thing before with rock

climbers and spelunkers. I've just never been around to see it."

She slipped, knocking her head hard against the ladder before catching on with her free hand. Flynn's heart stopped and Kean sat down. "I can't watch. She's never going to make it, everybody in town's going to hate us. Probably tar and feather us for not taking care of our only doctor. Do they really tar and feather people anymore? It doesn't sound pleasant, whatever it is, and I'm really allergic to feathers."

"She's going to make it," Flynn said as much to Kean as to himself. "I don't know how, but she will, just like she's made it the other times. She's the most independent, bullheaded person I've ever met."

"Hell, she was probably an army colonel in her other life."

She swung her leg over onto the roof and crawled on all fours to Scully. Kean stood and thumped Flynn on the back. "Well, hot damn, she did it. I can't believe it. I gotta tell you I had my doubts."

Flynn let out a deep breath that felt as if it had come all the way from his feet. "I better light those flares. The chopper will be here soon."

Kean grinned. "And, thanks to the doc, we'll all see the next sunrise."

"Yeah." Flynn rubbed his leg as he headed for an open spot between the trees. "Never underestimate the gift of another sunrise."

"Or the determination of the local doc," Kean added as he followed. "She's something, isn't she?"

Flynn thought about that as he snapped the flares and

set them out. Their dense black smoke curled into the sky, marking the landing site. BJ Fairmont *was* something, always had been. She could make him angrier than anyone, defied him, and was hell-bent on doing things her way, not caring a rat's behind if he agreed or not.

Weren't woman supposed to mellow when they got older? Hell, BJ hadn't mellowed one bit. She was like a damn drill sergeant, ready to chew anyone's ass who got in her way.

THE NEXT MORNING, as he pushed open the white picket gate that led through the garden beside her house to the doctor's office entrance on the side, Flynn was still trying to figure out what the heck BJ Fairmont was all about. He'd thought he understood her well, would have staked his life on it. But times and BJ had changed, and now he wasn't sure. She was stronger, more self-assured, capable, in charge, a leader. She took care of this town no matter what the risk. He knew that responsible feeling, but never suspected BJ did.

She hated heights and she couldn't climb worth squat, and still she'd gone up on that roof after Scully. She'd stayed with him and gotten him stabilized till the airlift had arrived. Flynn hadn't even had a chance to say thanks.

A fountain gurgled somewhere inside the garden, and the scent of flowers drenched the air. Insects and birds darted about, and he'd never seen so many damn roses in his life. The pristine-white clapboard house with green gambrel roof and shutters and brown rabbit hopping across the yard made him feel as if he'd walked into one of those Jane Austen movies Grandma Mac liked to watch.

He'd bent to get a closer look at a white rose brushed with gray and purple, when a child's voice said, "If you wait till Doc BJ gets back she'll cut you a rose and wrap it in a wet paper towel so you can take it home and put it in a glass of water. It makes the whole room smell good. But you got to be real careful of the thorns because they hurt like hell if they stick you."

Flynn grinned. The sweet little voice had him till the *hell* part. Two little boys sat on a white bench by the house. About five and seven, he guessed, but he was no expert on kids, except for the hell-on-wheels glint in the older one's eyes. *That* he could relate to.

"I'm Drew and this is my little brother, Petey. He has diabetes and today he's got a splinter, too." He took his brother's finger and held it up for Flynn to see as he hunkered down by the boys.

Flynn shook his head. "That must hurt."

Petey nodded and Drew said, "Why do you have to walk with a cane?"

"Messed up my leg."

"Doc BJ can fix you right up. She can fix anything. This is Wednesday, so she's over at Ms. Millie's, making a house call, giving her vitamins and checking her blood pressure. Ms. Millie bakes no-sugar pudding for me and Petey, and we visit every afternoon and talk about stuff. Ms. Flo's the nurse. She'll be here about noon. Doc BJ has office hours late on Wednesdays for all the people who have to work."

Flynn chuckled. "You sure know a lot about Doc BJ." This was more personal information about BJ Fairmont than he'd had in twenty years. Her father had died some time ago and that she didn't still live with her mother surprised him. He'd always imagined Barbara Jean Fairmont in that big white-columned house on the hill at the edge of town. Strange that he never thought of her married, just single.

Drew said, "She watches Petey real close…'cause of his diabetes. We live around the corner with our aunt and come here every morning for breakfast. Petey already had a banana with peanut butter."

Drew pointed to the second floor. "She sleeps up there. Petey and I have a secret hideout under the kitchen window flower box and pretend this is a jungle. We can hear Doc BJ cooking in the kitchen and talking on the phone. Hideouts are fun."

"My brothers and I used to have a hideout up at Silver Gulch," Flynn said. "We found this little cave by the main entrance, hidden by brush and this pine tree with two trunks. We used to ride our bikes there."

Drew's eyes danced. "Petey and I have old bikes. Maybe we—"

"It's too far and I was a lot older. Your hideout sounds great, and it's close to the kitchen if you get hungry."

"Maybe Doc BJ will give you breakfast, too. The kitchen's in the back of her office," Drew said.

Flynn tried to remember the last time he'd eaten. His stomach growled and the boys laughed, their faces lighting up in youthful innocence. He thought of all the kids he'd seen in places not fit to raise cattle, much less children.

"Petey needs to get more exercise, so Doc BJ plays catch with us. She's awful at catch, even for a girl. She can't catch anything. She sucks!"

"Are you telling stories about me, Drew?" BJ asked from down the path.

Flynn stood and ruffled Drew's head, then Petey's. BJ looked great today. Climbing on roofs agreed with her. How could she be so fresh and bright after yesterday? It had to have taken a toll. But she'd not only met the challenge, she thrived on it. "Just *man* talk. You know how it is."

She eyed Flynn, her expression suddenly serious. Did she know about the *going-to-pot* idea? He wouldn't be surprised if she picked up a bird feeder and beaned him right there on the spot.

"I called the hospital an hour ago and Scully was okay. Should come home today. Has anything changed? Is that why you're here?"

"No." He mentally breathed a sigh of relief. He wasn't in the mood for a beaning. Yesterday had pretty much done him in. Today he wanted peace. "This is just a friendly visit. We can talk after you fix a certain splinter."

BJ turned her attention to the boys. "A splinter? Oh, my. I thought this was just a breakfast visit."

She gripped the boys' hands, one on each side. Her ability to care for people was remarkable. It came as natural to her as firing a rifle did to him. Which proved how opposite the two of them were.

He followed the little procession through double glass doors with original wood mullions and into a hall with buffed random-width oak floors, dark green walls and wide white trim. A reception desk occupied a corner by the doors; the waiting room was on one side of the hall and the examining rooms on the other.

The boys headed to a room with teddy-bear wallpaper, yellow curtains and a bear on a stool. Petey took the bear, then climbed onto the table like someone who'd done it many times.

Flynn leaned against the wall outside. Even kids were entitled to privacy.

He heard Drew say, "I'm still writing down everything Petey eats, but my spelling isn't good. That new sticker machine you got him for testing his blood sugar doesn't hurt much, does it, Petey? Aunt Katie said thanks for buying it for him."

"You're a really good big brother, Drew," BJ said. "You should be proud of yourself for helping Petey."

"Aunt Katie's got a new boyfriend *again* and we don't like him. He yells at us. Give Petey his insulin and then we can eat. That big guy with the cane who came in with us hasn't eaten, either. His stomach growled. Maybe we can all have bacon and eggs."

BJ laughed. A light, sincere sound that made Flynn smile. She might suck at catch, and her climbing ability put a serious crimp in the theory of man evolving from apes, but the woman sure as hell understood kids.

"If Colonel MacIntire would like to join us for bacon and eggs, he'd be most welcome," she said. "Though he really likes oatmeal. It's one of his favorite foods." Had she raised her voice a fraction for him, suspecting he was listening?

Drew asked, "Is he really a colonel? In the army and everything?"

"Yes, he is," BJ answered, then added, "now we'll give Petey his shot in the tummy and we'll all go eat. I made fresh peanut butter yesterday."

Shot in the tummy? Flynn peeked in the room as Petey lay down. He was five; there wasn't much tummy there to stick. But he didn't cry or complain or even whimper.

"All done," BJ said. "Time to eat."

BJ and the boys trooped out, nearly running into Flynn. Drew said, "Doc's fixing bacon and eggs. She makes great dippy ones you can dunk in the bacon. Do you want some? She said you liked oatmeal, but Petey can't have that because it's a carbohydrate."

"Actually, I was thinking more of…" *Black coffee and a couple of cigarettes* almost popped out of his mouth, till he caught BJ's eyes, which seemed to say, *Oh, please behave. Well, hell.* "Bacon and eggs are great, and I only like oatmeal served in a football helmet."

The boys laughed. And twenty minutes later they were still laughing as they ran out the back door.

"So," BJ asked as she collected dishes and he cleaned off the table. "What's with your *friendly* visit? Another lecture about climbing on roofs?"

"How bad's Petey's diabetes?"

"In kids, treating diabetes is a balancing act between insulin, food and exercise. Takes a lot of monitoring and special care. The boys live with their aunt. She got them when their mother and father died in a terrible car crash in the mountains two years ago. They've been through a lot, and Katie's young—twenty-five—and got a life of her own. Raising two boys, one a special-needs child, is not what she had in mind."

"You take care of a lot of people."

She scraped breakfast remains into the garbage disposal. "It's my job. You have yours—I have mine."

"Like caring for Scully and Kean?"

She stopped stacking plates in the dishwasher and quirked an eyebrow at him, as if she hadn't expected him to say that, either. "The MacIntire clan would have managed fine if I hadn't been there yesterday. They're a resilient lot. I just made things a little easier."

She went back to loading dishes, and he took her arm and turned her toward him. Her green eyes were a match for the perfect lawn outside the window; her skin was fresher than any flower in her garden. He spotted a red mark on her left temple, probably from when she'd knocked herself on the ladder going to get Scully. That was his own fault. If he wasn't tied to this damn cane, he'd have been the one on that roof, not her.

"We both know Scully was a little harried by the time the fire department got him down, and doing airlift and not facing a jarring two-hour ride to Billings in an ambulance helped a lot. That plan of yours for outdoing me worked fine."

"Scully on that roof was not part of any plan."

"You on that roof and not me seriously dented my

overinflated ego—that *is* what you called it, right? I wanted to thank you for yesterday, and if you think you can help with my leg, I'm willing to listen."

Okay, where the hell had that come from? That was not why he came. He'd wanted to say thanks, period. But now that the words were out…. "I can't let my brothers or anyone else down again. You're here and I'm here and why the hell not. I sure don't have anything else to do."

He pulled his wallet from his back pocket and drew out a blank check, then sat down at the kitchen table. "Okay, name your fee."

She stood perfectly still in the middle of her pristine yellow-and-white kitchen. "You're a soldier. You're paid in full. And I don't think my ideas will work. You need counseling, Flynn."

His body tensed. "I don't need counseling. I'm fine. And how'd you get so damn sure about what I need and don't need, and how'd you get so stubborn?"

"Went to school with some big Irishman. A total pain in the butt, but he taught me everything I know."

"You passed me up years ago, and I don't want your blasted pity, Fairmont, just your medical advice." He pulled out a pen. "How much?"

She shook her head, her long blond hair swaying across her slender shoulders. "I don't pity you, and for sure I'm not taking your money. Look, you've given twenty years of your life to—"

"Doing exactly what the hell I wanted to do." He straightened his spine. "I pay my way. I'm not a charity case, someone to be pitied."

"I never said I pitied you. I just don't take money from people who serve our country so I can live like this." She gestured at the kitchen. "I owe you."

He stood and jammed the pen and checkbook into his pocket. "Forget it. This was a dumb idea. I don't know what I was thinking. It's always got to be your way or no way."

"That's your motto, not mine."

He snagged his cane, which was hanging from the table edge. "Thanks for helping Scully. Stay off roofs. You could have killed yourself."

She tipped her chin. "I'll do whatever I want."

Her green eyes met his across the room. "Do you listen to anyone?"

"Do you?"

"Ah, screw it." He strode across the kitchen and out the back door.

Chapter Three

After evening office hours were over, BJ decided that this day had to be the longest in recorded history. Not only had it started with her battling with Flynn and being in the wrong *again*, but all her patients had wanted to know about it. They weren't sick; they'd craved juicy details. Today this wasn't a doctor's office but a blasted gossip mill. She had no idea how everyone had found out about her encounter with Flynn in the first place.

She set the lock, turned off the lights and spied Dixie jogging up the walk. *Dixie running? Oh, boy!* BJ undid the lock and opened the door, preparing herself for yet another catastrophe. "What's happened now?"

Dixie pulled up short. She tried to give BJ an indignant look while gasping for breath. "How do you know something happened? How do you know I haven't started exercising and decided to cut my fat intake the way you're always nagging me to do?"

"Because no pigs of any shape or size have flown through my garden or over my house tonight."

BJ laughed and Dixie spread her arms wide. "Just what I need—a smart-ass doctor for a friend. But that can wait. Right now Flynn's in a mess. Some cowboys were hitting on that new young barmaid, Belle, over at the Cut Loose, and Flynn knocked them out before anyone realized what happened. You should have seen it, like some Schwarzenegger movie."

BJ ran her fingers through her hair. "Damnation!"

"Hold on—there's more. To keep his bar from being turned into a pile of kindling, Ray called Jack. So, unless you want to see an army colonel and a Chicago cop go at it, you'd better think of something fast. I figure this is partly your fault, since everybody knows you and Flynn had words and he's been spoiling for a fight all night. That's not like him."

BJ closed her eyes and massaged her temples. "I don't believe this."

"That's why you're coming with me right this instance."

BJ barely got a chance to relock the door before Dixie grabbed her hand and tore down the garden path and out the gate. They rounded the corner and elbowed their way into the saloon. Four stunned men lay on the floor, Jack on one side of the room, Flynn on the other, eye to eye, testosterone dripping from the walls. Men!

"See? What did I tell you!" Dixie whispered.

She couldn't stand here and wait patiently while things went to hell. And Dixie was right. This was partly her fault for not helping Flynn on his terms instead of insisting things go her way. What had happened to kindness and understanding? She was one stubborn woman and this was the result. Why hadn't she just taken his damn check and donated the money to charity or something? She wasn't any more mature now than she had been in high school. *Grow up, BJ!*

BJ walked into the middle of the room and stood between Jack and Flynn. His legs were apart, lip bloody, face pinched into hard lines. He looked as mean and ornery and dangerous as a wounded bear. Even in battle mode, though, he looked more handsome than any man should.

He growled, "Get the hell out of here, Fairmont. Go write a prescription."

"I'm not going anywhere, MacIntire." She pointed to the men on the floor, who were too stunned to move. "Who do you think's going to stitch these guys back together—Martha Stewart? *Me,* that's who, and I'm already tired and had a long enough day without you adding to it."

He clenched his hands and nodded at the cowboys on the floor. "They were asking for it."

And knowing Flynn, they probably were. "Well, you're not a one-man vigilante committee."

She faced Jack. "This is all my fault."

Jack cocked an eyebrow. "I doubt that."

Flynn gave a dry laugh and added, "You sure as hell didn't take these guys out."

BJ ignored Flynn and continued. "If I patch these men up and assume responsibility for the big ugly one still standing, will you let him go with me and not lock him up?"

Jack gave her a half smile. "You figure you can pull that off?"

Flynn snorted. "This I gotta see."

BJ turned back to him, staring him dead in eyes lit with the fire of fight. He had great eyes, the kind that opened clear through to his troubled soul. "Listen up, MacIntire. You can either come with me and mind your manners, or I'll get Grandma Mac in here to read you the riot act. It's your call. What's it going to be?"

She watched the color in his eyes darken to navy and the fire die. He understood what she said. Grandma Mac was not to be messed with, either out of respect for the woman who'd known every kid in town for the past fifty years, or maybe because no one wanted to disappoint her. And she would still keep wayward males in line with a few choice phrases that seemed to bring them to their senses and make them shape up.

Flynn held out his hand to one of the cowboys on the floor and said, "Apologize to Belle and we'll call it even."

The cowboy gave Flynn a wary look, took his hand and stood. The other three men did the same and the crowd slowly dispersed to reclaim bar stools and tables, the usual din gradually filling the room.

Jack ran his hand around his neck and said to BJ, "Good luck, you're going to need it. Call me if you want help. Flynn's a hell of a good guy. He's going through a bad patch. Just wish he wouldn't take it out on the town."

Jack left and BJ watched Flynn hand Ray money, probably for the bar bill and damages. That was more the Flynn MacIntire she knew, a man who accepted responsibility for his actions. The fighting side was one she hadn't seen at all.

Flynn, cane in hand, followed the cowboys to the door, but when he passed her, BJ snagged his arm and held him back. His muscles were firm, powerful. "You're really coming with me without a battle? Did you get hit in the head or something?"

FLYNN STUDIED her slim hand in his. It seemed defenseless, but that was a lie. Barbara Jean Fairmont was one of the strongest, most resilient people he'd ever met, even if she did drive him nuts. Still, she wasn't invincible, as she thought he was. "You really believe I'd let you go off alone with four cowboys who just gave another woman a hard time?"

She wrinkled her nose and tsked. "If that's what gets you to my office, fine. But nothing's going to happen to me. Everyone keeps the doctor safe. Without me, the closest medical care is an hour's drive unless you want to visit Doug Lambert at the veterinary clinic."

He slid his arm away, and grabbed her elbow and ushered her out of the saloon. "The sooner you get those cowboys patched up, the sooner you can get some sleep. You look like hell."

"You're such a flatterer. How can I ever resist your manly charms?" she said with so much sarcasm that he chuckled. It felt good, damn good. Even better than the fight.

"Do you have to walk so fast?" she groused. "Slow down a little, will you?"

"Hell, I'm the one with the cane, Fairmont. Keep up." He turned into her garden and saw the cowboys waiting by the side door. She pulled up to them, lifted a flowerpot and snatched a key.

She directed the cowboys to the examining room, then leveled Flynn a stern warning. "Just for the record, you *are* spending the night on my sofa like I promised. I gave Jack my word, so get used to it."

Her gaze met Flynn's. Both of them squared off, as if seeing who'd back down first. "It's stupid to sleep on your couch when I have a bed at home," he said.

"What's stupid is you slugging it out with those poor cowboys because you're pissed off at me for not doing what you wanted this morning."

His eyes widened. "What's with the poor cowboy bit? Those guys are younger than me, stronger and they have six good legs between them."

She put her hands on her hips. "You're built like a grizzly, have the same temperament and have probably been in more bar fights than Jesse James. The cowboys didn't stand a chance. The reason I came after you is that I didn't feel like gluing you *and* Jack back together after you made mincemeat out of each other. And, if you messed up Jack's face for his wedding, Maggie would strangle you with her bare hands."

BJ flipped on the light in the hallway and nodded at a couch in the dark waiting room. "Stay there and let me deal with the cowboys. Then I'll see if your lip needs stitches and check out your eye—it's starting to swell. Don't break anything in my house because you're in a nasty mood."

"I'm going home."

"No you're not. You got yourself into this. Now you

can live with the consequences." She turned and left him standing in the hallway.

"You're not telling me what to do, Fairmont," he called after her.

"You're not going out and causing another round of mayhem. I'm all mayhemed out." She didn't even dignify his statement with a glance back. She was used to everyone doing what she said without question. *Well, not him, dammit.*

He watched her go into one of the examining rooms, then come out with two ice bags and a towel. "For the lip and eye. Don't put the ice directly on your eye. Wrap the bags in the towel. If you're hungry you know where to find the kitchen. Clean up after yourself. This isn't the Waldorf."

He looked from the ice bags and the towel, suddenly realizing he was tired to the bone. Tired of fighting, tired of not being able to walk, tired of his own miserable company, which was not improving one bit. And no matter what BJ said, he wasn't leaving her alone in the middle of the night with men he didn't know.

Flynn went to the leather sofa and dropped onto the soft cushions, his cane propped against his left knee. It *was* better than jail and way better than a lecture from Grandma Mac. She'd raised him to be a gentleman. Tomorrow he'd bring her flowers and apologize.

He listened to BJ's voice drifting out from the examining room as she gave the cowboys hell about mistreating Belle. BJ Fairmont was good at giving hell. She didn't take crap from anyone, including him. She kept

Whistlers Bend in line as much as the sheriff did. And her word carried as much weight as the written law.

He needed food. He hadn't eaten since *dippy* eggs with the boys. His stomach rolled, the egg part not sounding too great right now, but maybe a sandwich would do the trick. He took his cane and headed for the kitchen, switched on the overhead light and opened the fridge. He pulled out turkey, ham and cheese and piled them high on fresh bread. Added a pickle, lettuce, some shredded carrots and green olives from a half-full jar. A masterpiece. His mouth watered.

He snagged a plate, then ripped a paper towel from the holder, knocking a pile of mail onto the floor.

He hunkered down and gathered the mail into a heap. Phone bill, electric bill, three advertisements for garden supplies, Washtash International Adoption Agency. He did a double take and pulled that envelope from the others, then placed the rest back on the counter. He sat at the table, bit into his sandwich, opened the envelope from the adoption agency and read.

"What the hell do you think you're doing?" BJ stood in the doorway, seething and pointing to the letter on the table.

He held up his sandwich. "Eating?"

She whipped the letter from his fingers. "Is nothing sacred to you? This is none of your business."

His gaze met her pissed-off one. "Me at the Cut Loose wasn't any of your damn business and that sure as hell didn't stop you from jumping in with both feet and giving me grief."

She tossed her hair the way she always did when she

wanted to be right but wasn't. "Reading other people's mail is a federal offense. I...I should have you arrested."

He sat back in the chair and took another bite of sandwich, feeling better now that he had food and BJ around to talk to. She settled him, made him feel he could succeed no matter what.

"Before you call in the feds," he said around a mouthful, "I have an idea that might help us both." He nodded at the chair across from him. "Besides, you're too tired to call the feds, and you probably don't even know the number. Sit down."

She closed her eyes for a moment and her shoulders sagged in defeat. "Why do I even bother with you?"

"My charismatic personality."

Her eyes snapped open. "That is *definitely* not it."

She parked herself in a chair and rested her head between her hands, elbows propped on the table, and looked at him as he said, "Here's the way things stand. You can help me get my leg in shape, but you won't let me pay."

He paused, waiting for her to bring up the counseling bit. When she didn't, he asked, "You're not going to tell me I need to talk to someone?"

"What do you mean, MacIntire?"

"I've been thinking about this. We both have something that the other needs. What if we barter?" He moved his sandwich her way. "I do something for you—you do something for me."

She yawned. "And what do you think you can do for me? Read the rest of my mail? Sack my refrigerator again?"

"I have a better idea."

"I'm breathless with anticipation. Whatever can it be?"

"Barbara Jean Fairmont, I'm going to marry you."

"SURE YOU ARE. That's the craziest thing you've ever said." BJ quirked her left eyebrow, She didn't have enough energy to quirk the right side, too. "You must have a concussion. You're delusional. How many fingers am I holding up?"

"None. They're on the side of your face. You help me get the use of my leg back and get fit for the army. I marry you and that *ups* your chances to adopt the baby *you* want. At least, that's what I got from the letter I just read. The fact that you're single is not helping your cause."

"Marriage? Me? You?" She hung her head and laughed. "Just when I thought this day couldn't get any crazier, Flynn MacIntire proposes marriage.

"In case your long-term memory's taken a hit, I should remind you that we can't even be in the same room without all hell breaking loose."

A slow smile fell across his mouth. "There was a time, long ago, when we were in a room together, a car together, the woods together, and got along real well."

Her eyes met his. "Like you said, long ago."

"But it did happen." Both were quiet for a moment, as if they were caught in a time warp, remembering the good times. And they were both aware just how good, how fresh, how exciting they were. He swallowed, then continued, "But this isn't a real marriage. It's a paper one. A formality. No one even has to know we're hitched except the adoption agency. I'll be around for a while for interviews and I can scrounge up some letters of recommendation from my army file."

"I'm glad you have that all figured out, but there is a child involved. What do we tell him or her?"

"The absolute truth. You and I got married to give the kid a better life. I'm gone a lot, but when I am home I'll acquaint myself with the child. I can't raise one—hell, I have no idea how to do that—but I can be there as a kind of safety net in case the kid needs something."

Flynn put down his sandwich and gave her a sincere look. "I've been all over the world, BJ. I've seen more war orphans and abandoned kids than you can imagine, living in abominable situations. If you can just save one, just one, I'm all for it. After the adoption is final, we get a divorce as easily as we got married. Sign some more papers and it's over. You have a baby—he or she has a great life. We're saving a life. That matters to me more than you can imagine."

Those words hit her hard. He'd seen so much death, and now there was a chance to give life. She understood that more than most. It was something they shared. Who would have thought all those years ago that they'd be having this conversation now and connecting over something like this. "But it doesn't seem very honest."

"Keeping a child in an overcrowded, understaffed orphanage where he doesn't even see the sun shine, when he could be with you in Whistlers Bend, is infinitely worse. We go into Billings tomorrow, get the license and have some judge in a little town on the way back marry us."

She massaged her temples. "Flynn, this is all very

noble of you, but the bottom line is you don't need me to get better. You can go back to Walter Reed. They have the best doctors, the best staff, the best of everything. I'm a small-town doctor without a lot of the facilities that could help you."

"You're a fine doctor—ask anyone around here. Besides, I can't do the hospital thing again." He swallowed. "No more."

And she knew better than to push him this time. He'd had enough and should do things his own way, *just as she did things her way.* How could two people be so alike and yet so different?

"When I couldn't help Scully on that roof I decided I had to do something. It was a wake-up call to get my ass in gear. I can't change what happened to the guys who were with me on that convoy, but I can change *me,* or at least try. I can be of service again. If I sit back and do nothing the enemy wins. That's what they're counting on."

She held out her hands, palms up. "I can't guarantee your leg will be good as new, Flynn. I have some techniques and can confer with other doctors and get their opinions, but—"

"And maybe something else will come up and you still won't be able to adopt," he said. "The one thing I know for damn sure is nothing's for damn sure. I bet you have a current blood test. There's no waiting period to marry in Montana. Is it a deal? You can't change that you're forty and you can't change that you're a doctor, but two parents instead of a single mom would help improve your chances for adoption a lot."

"And maybe you'll get better and get back to the army." Wasn't this the original plan—to get Flynn out of her life? Now the plan just had a glitch. Marriage. Some glitch!

He held out his hand to shake hers.

She studied it and said, "I can't believe I'm doing this."

"Everybody wins, BJ. No downside."

She nodded and shook his hand firmly. Her heart speeded up. "Tomorrow we're getting married."

He smiled at her, the same kind of smile he used to give her over twenty years ago that made her dizzy and weak. It had the same effect now. She let go of his hand. "We are. We should get some sleep."

He stood and she said, "I left a pillow and sheets on the sofa."

She eyed his sandwich, piled with all kinds of really delicious stuff. Suddenly, she was starved. Wasn't there something about joint ownership in a marriage? He started to bite into the rest of his sandwich, she grabbed it right out of his fingers and took a bite. She closed her eyes. "Oh, this is really incredible, MacIntire."

"Yeah, and it was mine."

"Was," she said, her mouth stuffed. She wiped her mouth on her shirttail and his eyes widened.

"Does your mother know you do that?"

"Husbands can't snitch on their wives. It's against the law. I'm too tired to get a napkin." She devoured the sandwich in five bites. "That was good. That was really, really good." She burped.

He stared and blinked to make sure he hadn't imagined what had just happened. "I've never seen anyone eat so fast in my life."

"You weren't a resident on eighteen-hour shifts. I should check your lip and your eye."

"I'm eating—*at least, I was*—so my lip's fine. And I see you licking mustard off your left thumb, so my eye must be okay, too."

She went to the sink and washed her hands, then came back to him and pointed to the chair. "Sit."

"Anyone ever tell you your bedside manner sucks?"

"After midnight I have no manners. It's the real me. Deal."

He did as she directed, and she placed her hands on his cheeks and angled his face up toward hers. *Big mistake.* The warmth of his skin against her palms set her totally on fire.

Usually, she had some willpower to ward off this sort of reaction to Flynn, to keep herself in check. But it was late and she had no willpower, especially with her touching him. That had never been the case before. The intimate feel of his five-o'clock shadow on her fingers and the firm set of his determined jaw…. So male, so virile. It had been a while since she'd encountered virile. Whistlers Bend was not match.com.

She took her hands away and pulled in a few deep breaths to get herself under control. He asked, "Are you okay?"

"Peachy." He needed a shower, but there was no way she'd survive thinking about Flynn MacIntire naked in her bathroom. "Look at the light."

She moved her hand over his eyes, watching the pupils dilate. And then she was watching more of him—how his eyes were clear and true, rimmed with black and lit with fire. She'd seen that fire before, though they'd never acted on it. But now… Every fiber of her body wanted to act. She mentally gave her head a shake to bring herself back to the moment. "Any pain in your eye?"

"I'm fine."

Too bad she wasn't, and now she had to touch his lip. *Holy cow.* To be attracted to Flynn from afar was one thing, but now she had to endure physical contact of the mouth variety. *And when she helped with his leg there'd be more physical contact.* Lots more. The only salvation was that the contact would be for short intervals, then he'd go back to his house and she'd have a chance to gain control of herself before he returned the next day.

She braced herself for touching him now. Felt his lip, warm and full and smooth against her fingers. Remembered kissing him for the first time and how she'd traced his lips with her fingers before she'd tasted them. *Oh, she wanted another taste now.*

His breath fell gently over her hand. "You're fine."

He gazed at her. "Well, you're not. You look like you have a fever."

"The sandwich must have made me sick."

"I'm the king of sandwiches. If anything's wrong it's because you gobbled it down like a truck driver and you're tired. Consider taking in a partner. You're swamped here and could use a break, Fairmont."

She dropped her hands to his neck and applied a little pressure. "Never tell the doc what to do after midnight. She tends to get cranky."

How could she want to kiss him one minute and do him bodily harm the next? Because he was Flynn MacIntire, that was why. "I don't need a damn partner."

"Did you just say *damn?*"

Maybe she should wring his neck after all. "And I am not slowing down." She turned her back to him and headed for the hallway. "See you in the morning."

FLYNN LOOKED AT his empty plate. She'd eaten the whole blasted sandwich, hadn't left him one crumb. He'd had only three bites and there was no more meat or cheese or bread. He opened the fridge and found an apple. Hell of a replacement for Sandwich-by-Flynn. Tomorrow he'd restock her food supply, maybe make the boys one of his special subs. He'd have to watch what he put on it because of Petey's diabetes. Maybe ham and cheese roll-ups would be okay.

He wandered into the waiting room and snapped the sheets she'd left for him over the sofa, then lay down. The moon cast shadows on the floor and ceiling as he thought about his almost wife. Why hadn't BJ married and had kids? She loved kids, was attractive, though bossy as hell and intimidating as an army tank. And she had that irritated look about her when she got hacked off. But there was a vulnerability lurking below the surface, just as there had been all those years ago. That hadn't changed at all.

He closed his eyes, still thinking about Barbara Jean as he drifted off to sleep, and slept till he heard, "Colonel? Wake up, Colonel." Someone poked his ribs.

It didn't sound like one of his men; besides, they knew better than to poke the Bear. Flynn pried open his eyes and gazed into two big brown eyes peering down at him.

Petey grinned. "I thought you died. You smell kinda dead. But I'm glad you didn't. I don't like it when people die and leave me behind. It's morning, Colonel. Why are you sleeping on Doc BJ's sofa? She told me to come get you for breakfast."

Flynn pushed himself up and gazed around. He'd slept through the night, the *whole night*. Something he hadn't done since he'd gotten stateside. He ran his hand over his head, trying to clear the fog from his brain. He felt grubby and obviously smelled worse. "Tell Doc BJ I'll catch up with her later, that I'm heading back to my house."

"She's not going to like it," Petey said in a little singsong voice. "She'll get *that* look."

Flynn smiled. "Yeah, I know *that* look. How are you doing this morning? How are you feeling?" he asked.

Petey glanced around as if he didn't know what Flynn meant. "I'm okay." He bit his bottom lip, then asked very politely, "And how are you feeling today, Colonel MacIntire?"

"I'm fine, Petey."

The little boy grinned again. "Doc BJ said that's manners, how you're supposed to talk to older people in civilized society." He scrunched up his little-boy face. "What's civilized society?"

Flynn felt a sense of pure delight in such innocence, followed by a twinge of panic. He couldn't think of a good definition of civilized society for a five-year-old. Hell, he couldn't think of a good definition for a forty-year-old. "It's when people treat one another kindly and use nice words so everybody gets along."

Petey nodded. "I think I like civilized society." He assumed a grown-up posture and held out his hand for Flynn to shake. "It's been nice talking to you today, Colonel MacIntire. I'll tell Doc BJ you're not staying for breakfast and not to get her panties in a twist." He shrugged. "That's what Deputy Roy always says about people if they're mad."

Flynn watched Petey skip his way back down the hall. The twisted-panties crack probably set civilized society back a century or two, but what a kid! Petey could charm the stripes off a sergeant and not even realize he was doing it, just as he didn't realize his diabetes was a problem. He dealt with it every day and went on. Flynn MacIntire could learn coping skills from a five-year-old.

Flynn folded the sheet, then put them and the pillow in the corner. He'd grab a shower and dress and be back here within the hour, then he and Barbara Jean Fairmont could get going to Billings.

And he made it back to her house with minutes to spare, thankful Grandma Mac was at her tae kwon do class or she'd hammer him with questions about getting dressed up in the middle of the day. Homey noises came from the kitchen and he headed there. He caught a glimpse of BJ in a pale pink suit as she darted by the entrance, and he paused in the doorway, taking her in. Her hair was braided around the back of her head in a sophisticated fashion, she wore pearl earrings and neck-lace, and her makeup was perfect. She was stunning, captivating. She knocked the breath right out of his lungs, making him glad he could lean against the door-jamb. He'd seen her lovely like this before, at the junior prom. She'd worn pink then, too. Flowers in her hair. So beautiful…like now.

"Nice—" He was about to say *wedding duds,* then saw Petey and Drew sitting on bar stools at the counter by the open kitchen window. Flynn grinned. "Hi, guys."

BJ handed Petey a black bag and ignored Flynn. She seemed nervous. He'd never seen BJ Fairmont that way. She was always in control.

"Here's your insulin. Be sure you tell Aunt Katie to put it in the fridge and to test your blood sugar before lunch, since I won't be around to do it today. Remind her this is important. I already talked to her once on the phone, but tell her again. She's not working, but in case she gets called in tell the babysitter to check you. If you have any problems call Flo. Her number's in the case."

Drew looked from BJ to Flynn. "Are you two going somewhere? You're all dressed up."

Flynn nodded. "I have a friend in Billings I want BJ to meet. It's…business."

Drew's eyes narrowed. "Doc BJ never goes any-where. She has to be here to take care of the town. That's why she has all those roses. It's her hobby while she's waiting around for people to get sick. Why would she go with you on business to Billings?"

"It's adult business that needs to be attended to today," BJ said in her doctor voice, which made what she said gospel. "And don't worry about me. Just remember to watch out for Petey." She kissed Petey on the top of the head, then Drew. "I'll be back by dinnertime to check your insulin then, Petey."

Drew nodded, looking again from Flynn to BJ. He said, "You guys are up to something." Then he took his brother's hand and walked down the hall, and they left out the double glass doors.

Flynn waited a beat to make sure the kids weren't coming back. "Damn, that was close." He sat on the bar stool by the window where Drew sat earlier. BJ scurried about, straightening the kitchen. "I almost called your suit wedding duds. If Grandma Mac got wind of this wedding… Well, to her a marriage is a marriage. She'd never understand it was just on paper."

BJ put the milk in the fridge. "My mother would have a conniption."

"I'm that bad a choice, huh?"

"It's not you. It's the elopement that would frost her cookies. Something like that out of the blue would not be acceptable, and I'd hear about it at every opportunity for the rest of my natural life. You weren't around the last time I almost got married. Fourteen bridesmaids, a carriage, doves, fifty yards of chiffon." She shuddered. "Looked like the circus had come to town. Mother loves the pizzazz."

"And you don't?"

She faced him. "My idea of pizzazz is bananas on my cereal."

Flynn came to her and cupped her shoulders in his palms. "You sure you still want to do this? You seem a little uptight, Doc."

She grinned, more relaxed now. A devilish grin, something he'd never seen on the straitlaced town doc. "Last night I maxed out my credit card online at Babies R Us, Mother and Infant, Gymboree and Little Tots."

He could only imagine what dollar amount that was for one of the wealthiest women in town. "Don't you think you're jumping the gun a little?"

Her big green eyes darkened a shade. "I always thought that I'd marry, and then I didn't and my practice consumed my life. Suddenly, I'm forty, and I want a baby more than ever. Giving a baby in a third-world country a good home really appeals to me, Flynn. I can't wait."

Flynn nodded. "Then let's get going before something happens and all our plans get shot to hell."

LATE-AFTERNOON SHADOWS stretched across BJ's garden as she walked up the path. She was exhausted. Getting married to Flynn MacIntire would exhaust anyone. Not just the drive, but they'd argued politics, art, books and everything else all the way to and from Billings. How could he be a Republican? *Dear Lord, she'd actually married a Republican!* And how could he not *like* Picasso and like Salvador Dali? She opened the side door—had she forgotten to lock it? Entered and came face-to-face with Maggie and Dixie standing in the hallway.

She glanced from one to the other, neither looking thrilled to see her. "What are you two doing here?"

"How could you?" Maggie seethed, her eyes little slits, her face flushed.

"How could I what?"

The phone rang and Dixie said as she jabbed her finger at it, "It's your mother. She's called every ten minutes for the past six hours. Grandma Mac's in a state. I think she's going to take Flynn out and shoot him dead."

"What are you two talking about?" BJ asked in a lighthearted tone, though prickles of panic danced along her spine. "Is there a problem?"

"Problem? Problem!" Dixie pursed her lips, tapped her foot and pointed to BJ's suit. "That's an understatement. How could you go and marry Flynn MacIntire and not tell us?"

Chapter Four

BJ nibbled her bottom lip and glanced from Maggie's furious face to Dixie's. How'd the best-kept secret in town leak out? *Because it wasn't the best-kept secret!* "It's not what you think. There's an explanation."

Dixie pointed at BJ with her index finger. "Only one thing matters—are you married to Flynn MacIntire or are you not?

"But—"

"Are you?"

She brushed Dixie's accusing finger away. "Yes, but it's not because we love each other. It's—"

"Lust!" Dixie's eyebrows shot so far up her forehead they disappeared into her hair. "I knew it when you came out of that saloon that something was up between you two. I told you sex should be involved, and then it was and you didn't even tell me. Some friend."

"This is one of those marriages built on sex?" Maggie added. "At forty? Who would have thought. Guess there are worse reasons to marry, and you're a woman with needs. Though you never mentioned any needs to me."

"*I do not have needs!* Well, I do, but not with Flynn MacIntire."

Maggie winked. "He's a handsome man, and if you come up with a way to keep from killing each other, the sex should be good. But why not tell Dixie and me?"

BJ threw her hands in the air. "The marriage is not over lust. It's over a baby."

Maggie's eyes widened. "Flynn MacIntire's going to be the father of your baby?"

"Well, sort of. That's one way of looking at it, but—"

"You didn't tell us about that, either! That's worse than the lust explanation."

"Will you just forget lust? It has nothing at all to do with this marriage. It's because of the baby, and it happened fast and—"

"You're *already* pregnant?"

"Ohforgodssake. I'm not pregnant!"

Maggie's eyes rounded to the size of cotton balls and Dixie said, "We didn't know you two were seeing each other, and now there's a baby *on the way*."

"But—"

"No buts."

"*Listen to me!*" BJ glared at Dixie, then Maggie and hissed, "This marriage is because I want to adopt, and marrying Flynn will expedite the matter. The one thing in life we agree on is there are children who deserve a good home. That's all there is to it. A paper marriage for an adoption. Done, finished, end of irate conversation. Go home."

Maggie hissed back, "The bottom line is you've been seeing Flynn MacIntire behind our backs, didn't tell us diddly and then ran off and got married without so much as a phone call to either of us to tell us what you were up to or to include us in your plans. You do realize what a big deal a marriage is around here. This isn't Vegas!"

"Yes, I do know, and that's precisely why we told no one. Everyone would turn it into something more than it is, and it's not the town's or your business!"

Oh, heck! Of all the things to say, that wasn't it. Telling best friends your business wasn't theirs was heresy. Amazing the trouble you would get into when you were tired to the bone and you had a big mouth.

Dixie's jaw dropped in astonishment. "Well," she huffed, "if *that's* the way you feel."

"I'm sorry. That's not what I meant."

"Yes, it is." She snagged Maggie by the sleeve and pulled her toward the door. "How could you do this after all we've been through together, BJ? We fished you out of the lake when you almost drowned. We taught you how to dance…well, we tried. We've done everything together, but now…"

"Can't you cut me some slack here?"

"No!" they said together. Dixie yanked open the door, and Flynn stood on the other side.

"You!" Dixie said on a gasp. "How could you marry BJ and not tell your family. Your brothers and Grandma Mac are in a frenzy."

Flynn stroked his chin. "I know. Boy, do I know!"

Dixie shook her finger. "And they have every right to be mad as hell, because we are, too."

She pulled herself up to all five foot three inches of

outrage. "In fact, I'm not sure when any of us will speak to either of you again." She glared at Flynn. "See if I ever save you the last piece of lemon meringue pie. I'd feed it to stray cats first."

She raised her chin even higher, stepped around Flynn and exited onto the sidewalk. The last rays of sunlight fell across the garden as Dixie and Maggie marched down the path. On a normal day this was BJ's favorite time, peaceful, content, contemplative. *Well, not tonight, Skippy!*

She looked at Flynn. "What the heck are you doing here? The two of us together have stirred up enough pandemonium. We need a break—about ten years' worth."

He let out a sigh and leaned against the doorjamb. "Grandma Mac threw me out."

BJ felt her mouth gape. She quickly shut it. "We've been back ten minutes. What did you do now?"

"What do you think? I married you! Me living anyplace other than *with you* is out of the question, at least as far as Grandma Mac and Scully and Kean are concerned. They're sure my soul's condemned to hell for all eternity already because I was off and married without family present. Still, a marriage took place, and she's not about to let me forget it. According to the lecture I just got, my place is with you."

Oh, no! Not this! BJ's stomach rolled. She hadn't planned on Flynn's being in the same town. Now the same address? *No way!* "But I don't want you."

His left eye twitched. "You really believe I want you?" He stroked his jaw, dark with the need for a shave. "But we are married. You've got me—I've got you. Package deal. If I tried to bunk in with someone else, my dear old grandmother would haul my sorry ass back here. I'm too tired to deal with ass hauling."

"Didn't you explain why we did this?"

He gave a dismissive shrug. "And I had about as much success as you apparently did explaining this marriage to Dixie and Maggie."

He raked his hairless head with his fingers, suddenly seemed as tired as she felt. "Hell, Fairmont! How'd this happen? Did you tell anyone?"

"Of course not. Did you?"

"Why would I? But someone found out someway. How did such a simple idea turn into a mess like this? It's just a marriage of convenience. Why don't any of them get that?"

"On some level they do—at least, Dixie and Maggie. But they're honked off I didn't keep them in the loop. Your family is another matter. A marriage is sacred especially as far as Grandma Mac's concerned. It's not something to be entered into lightly."

BJ leaned against the other side of the doorjamb and took him in. The fading sun bathed him in a golden glow. His mussed dress shirt was open at the throat, his tie loose around his neck. Too handsome, too male, too close. *And about to get a whole lot closer!*

Usually, she saw Flynn in the distance, which made it easier to get over her attraction, because when they weren't together or even in eyesight of each other, she could remind herself the attraction was stupid, dumb, idiotic.

But this hadn't been a short day. There'd been no

time to remember that the attraction made no sense. She took in his fine build and the attraction made all kinds of sense. *She needed to get over it.* "So, now what do we do?"

"There's a choice?"

She didn't like the sound of that, and he gave her a "don't be thickheaded" look. "I live with you till we get this adoption thing through or I get back in the army, whichever comes first."

She stood straight and held out her hands as if warding off the devil himself. *"No way.* I hate arguing and yelling and fighting. Most of the time that's all we do."

"We're going to be roomies, Dr. Fairmont. Get used to it."

"We'll kill each other."

"We didn't always want to do that." And they both knew exactly what that meant. They'd had good times together, fun times, romantic times…once upon a time.

"I'm talking about today. I almost threw you out of the car on more than one occasion, and I thought, when the car slowed down, you wanted to do the same to me. Now you want to live together? Are you crazy?"

"We'll have to get along. Then we'll divorce, the way we planned. The only thing's that's changed is where we live. It's probably a blessing—"

"Wanna bet?"

"The adoption agency might smell a rat if they checked up on us and we *weren't* living together."

BJ closed her eyes for a second. How could she get out of this one? "There has to be some other way, right?"

"Are you going to throw me into the street? Bad omen for a new marriage."

"Okay, there isn't a way out." She'd survive living with him by remembering all the reasons she disliked him so intensely. By thinking of what they disagreed on…which wouldn't be a problem, because it happened to be everything. Whenever he opened his big mouth it would distract her from any and all attraction she had for Flynn MacIntire. She smiled.

"You're okay with this?"

"I'm getting there. Collect your things and I'll check the guest room. Tomorrow we get started on a regimen for your leg."

"To get me back into the army?"

"We're both motivated. In fact, the longer we live together I bet the more motivated we'll get, and you'll be back with your brigade or unit or whatever in no time."

He nodded. "It's a plan." He turned to leave, and came face-to-face with—

"Mother?" BJ felt her head start to spin. *Could this day get any worse?*

Her mother stood tall and gazed from one to the other. "I'm certain you two have many plans. Sharing some of them with the rest of us would have been considerate."

Margaret Fairmont, her auburn hair fashionably streaked and styled in a short sophisticated bob that set off her green eyes, her chestnut Gucci bag matching her shoes, her silk cream blouse and tan slacks completing the ensemble, was perfectly furious.

"Barbara Jean, how could you do this to me?"

"Mother, this isn't personal. We didn't tell anyone

because it's not a real marriage, and we didn't want to give anyone the impression it was."

"You stood in front of an official and swore to take each other for life. You are both rational, intelligent adults, so this is indeed a marriage." She glared at Flynn, her eyes lit with fire "And how could you do this to Grandma Mac? A truly wonderful lady. I expected better from you."

Flynn straightened, looking very dignified, a man in charge. "Mrs. Fairmont, I assure you I meant no disrespect to you or my grandmother. And don't fault BJ. This was my idea and—-"

"And I agreed," BJ added as she stood beside him. Flynn was not taking the fall for this. "I want to adopt, Mother. I want to give a child a good loving home, and Flynn's agreed to marry me to make that possible. He did it for me."

"And BJ's helping me with my leg."

Margaret glanced from one to the other, some of the fire leaving her eyes. "Well, there are many reasons for marriage, and you seem to have found yours. I've arranged for a reception at the country club the day after tomorrow to give this marriage an air of propriety. You will both be there for your families. If you do intend to adopt, then the child should be given the benefit of two responsible parents."

She turned on her heel and walked down the garden path. BJ turned to Flynn, "Well, Flynn MacIntire, welcome to the family."

TAKING HIS LIFE in his hands, Flynn kissed Grandma Mac on the cheek, grabbed his two duffels and closed the door to the MacIntire house behind him. *Holy hell!* He'd left many times before—usually, when his leave had ended, and he was heading back to some war zone or battle thousands of miles away. This time his house constituted the war zone and Grandma Mac had won the battle. Living with his new wife was not an option, no matter how many times he tried to explain the situation.

He threw his stuff into the back seat of the rental car and drove the two blocks over to BJ's. He parked on the street, the last rays of sunlight fading behind the mountaintops, the streetlights winking on. He stared at the gambrel-roofed house. The lamppost by the garden entrance illuminated the Dr. Barbara Jean Fairmont plaque and the walkway in case someone needed help at night. Lamps glowed in the open upstairs windows, curtains ruffling in the evening breeze. His new address…at least, for a while.

He slung one duffel over his shoulder, snatched the other in his left hand and his cane in the right. He made his way up the walk to the back door, opened it and went inside.

BJ came down the hallway from the kitchen. "Where have you been? I thought maybe you changed your mind."

"My mind has nothing to do with this. Grandma Mac saw fit to remind me *again* of her displeasure over our elopement and her exclusion. Guess we can't avoid that reception at the country club."

"And live? My mother? Your grandmother? Dixie and Maggie? If we tick them off anymore they'll stake us out for the vultures."

She'd changed into soft jeans and a yellow sweat-shirt. Her hair was pulled back, gathered at her neck with a matching ribbon. Everything about her was perfectly pressed and fitted, except her shoes. BJ Fairmont barefoot? The millionth surprise of the day. "I never thought I'd be moving into some woman's house."

"I'm not some woman. I'm your…"

"Wife? Couldn't get it out? I know what you mean." He took in the quiet house. "I should be at the Cut Loose, swilling beer and dragging on cigarettes."

"Be my guest, but don't even think about smoking in here. Outside, in the far corner, maybe by the compost pile is okay, I suppose, unless the wind blows this way. Ever consider giving up smoking?"

"I'll smoke in the garden. Your roses won't drop off the stem." Fatigue suddenly settled over him like a torrential downpour. He needed sleep and BJ had mentioned a guest room. "We'll deal with all this tomorrow. Where do I bunk in for night?"

"The *bunk's* upstairs, first door on the left. The bath's across the hall. Pick up after yourself. Ms. Eversole cleans on Tuesdays and Fridays and sometimes stops in to tidy up on other days."

"You have a cleaning lady? How sweet the rich life."

BJ gritted her teeth. "Ms. Eversole cleans the office every day. She needs the money and charity is out of the question. So, yes, I have a cleaning lady. Which means now *we* have a cleaning lady, which means this place stays neat so she doesn't have to work so hard."

"You clean for the cleaning lady?"

BJ eyed his duffels. "Are you going to get the rest

of your stuff, or stand here giving me advice on hearth and home?"

He toed his things. "This is it, Doc. The rest of my stuff."

She peered closer. "My *shoes* wouldn't fit in there." She nodded at the stairs. "I'll be up later. I have things to take care of for tomorrow's patients. If you need something there's an intercom on the hall wall, so you can reach me without yelling. Don't yell. I hate yelling."

He started to leave, then turned back. "Weren't you supposed to check on the boys tonight?"

"Here and gone. They don't know what to make of this marriage thing."

"They have a lot of company on that one, Doc." Flynn climbed the steps to the top and went left, entering...*the garden of eternal slumber? Flowers everywhere!* Blue ones on the wallpaper, yellow on bedspread, both woven into the carpet. The room even smelled like flowers. Flowers were fine, but...*this?*

He turned back into the hall and yelled from the top of the stairs, "BJ!"

She appeared at the bottom and raised both eyebrows while pursing her lips. "Intercom?"

"What am I supposed to do with that bedroom?"

"Sleep in it?" She put her hands to her hips. "I realize it's a little *girlie,* but trucks and cars and things that go and shoot and explode don't do it for me." Her mouth twisted with amusement. "My other guests have never complained. In fact, they love it."

"And how many of those other guests have been guys?"

She folded her arms. "Is that any of your business?"

He considered the question a minute. It wasn't his business, but for some reason he wondered. He gazed at her softness and her golden hair. His insides stirred, and he suddenly wondered a lot. "We *are* married. Maybe you should tell me."

"Eat dirt and die, MacIntire." She gave him a superior smirk. "Like you're going to tell me about all your female exploits?"

"Point taken."

"There's a small library across the hall and a living room at the end, but it has two love seats, not large enough to sleep on, especially you *and* your ego. You can use the couch in the waiting room again if that suits you, or the floor. You'll figure it out."

She left and he crossed the hall to the library. Books, antique desk, everything neat and orderly, but no place to sleep. He headed for the living room, passing BJ's room. He recognized it in an instant. Not just because of more flowers and its being the only bedroom left, but because of the worn oak rolltop desk he knew had been her father's. Flynn remembered going to Dr. Benjamin Fairmont when he was a kid. The man had died of cancer about twelve years ago. Rotten shame. Nice guy, terrific doctor, everyone thought so, especially his daughter.

A brass lamp illuminated pictures that covered the entire wall over the desk. Some were in frames; others were pinned to a corkboard. New pictures, old ones and everything in between.

He took down a photo of Grandma Mac, another of

his parents at his dad's retirement party, one of his grandfather, who'd been gone almost twenty years now.

"Do you always go through a woman's things?" BJ said as she came in.

"Only when I'm married."

"Keep this up and I'll be a widow."

He held out the picture of his grandfather. "A lot of these are from your dad."

BJ picked up the old photo and smiled as she looked at it. "Before good roads and airlifts. Dad was a one-man band around here." She put the picture back on the board. "When you bring someone into the world and care for them the rest of their life they're family." She nodded at the collection. "Guess they're part of my family, too."

She hitched her chin toward the doorway. "I put solid-green sheets on your bed and a brown magic marker on the nightstand. You can color them camouflage and sleep like a baby. And right now you can leave, because I'm going to bed. This day has been way too long already."

He picked up the photo of Snooky, Trixie and the twins that sat on the desk. "More family?"

A faraway expression came into her eyes as she absently ran her finger over the glossy picture. Fear swept over her face, but it left as fast as it had come. No one would have noticed unless they'd experienced that same feeling, and he'd been there more times than he wanted to think about. To have BJ experience it, too, jolted him. "What happened?"

She put the picture back on her desk and her eyes met

his through the dim light. She started to deny that anything had happened at all, then seemed to know he'd
never buy it. She let out a deep breath. "I could have lost
them. One baby breech, Trixie in a lot of pain. It was
raining like the devil, so air care was out of the question."

"What…what if you'd…?"

"If I'd lost them?" She closed her eyes for a second,
massaged her forehead, then looked back to him. "What
do you do?"

"I wish the hell I knew, Fairmont. God, I wish I
knew." He felt the words come from somewhere deep
inside.

"I'll tell you what my dad told me. Life isn't fair. All
we can do is try to even the odds." She kissed him on
the cheek, then she left, her bare feet barely audible on
the hallway carpet, the old steps creaking as she started
downstairs.

He followed her out into the hall. "What the hell's
that supposed to mean, Fairmont?" he yelled over the
banister, his voice echoing off the walls.

"That's for you to figure out."

"Thought doctors were so damn smart and had all the
answers."

She stopped at the bottom and gazed. "If I was so
damn smart and had all the answers, MacIntire, you
wouldn't be sleeping in my guest room." She gave him
a cheeky grin and faded from view.

"Well, big fat whooping hell," he said into the empty
hallway. He'd been looking for some insightful revela-
tion and all he'd gotten was double talk.

He tramped back to the guest room, grabbed his personal things from his duffel, then went into the frilly bathroom with lacy shower curtain and little jars of cream and shampoo and other bottles of goo on the counter. "Why does anyone need all this crap?"

He showered and wrapped himself in a towel he took off the bar. Not wrap, exactly, more like the fig-leaf approach. He caught his reflection in the big mirror over the sink. He'd bathed in strange places, makeshift showers in the field, a waterfall once, even deserted houses that had been abandoned in war. But never had he had a pink rose-print towel draped over his... How'd he get into this?

He crossed the hall to his room. Keeping the light off, he exchanged the towel for skivvies, peeled back the comforter and fell into bed, sinking into the pillow-top mattress. *Holy cow,* he'd died and gone to heaven, he was sure of it. His first aversion to the flowers had been more a reaction to the day and getting tossed out of his house than anything else.

He liked flowers. *This* was a little overkill, but so what. Right now he could sleep anywhere—at least, for a while, unless the damn dreams started.

He closed his eyes and drifted off, feeling the fatigue fade—until something woke him. A ringing phone somewhere far off? A voice? Someone moving around fast.

Trouble!

His eyes flew open, adjusting to the moonlight and zeroing in on a door across the room. Where'd he put his rifle? He jumped up and made for the door, yanked it open and collided full force with a woman, distress in her eyes. He shoved her behind him against the wall, protecting her, searching for the trouble.

"Flynn," She coughed and gasped his name. "You're squashing me."

Slowly, he turned and looked down at the woman. He did a double take. *"Fairmont?"*

Her eyes were wide as she asked, "What are you doing?"

He had no idea. Where the hell was he? He glanced around. Not a bunker or a truck or jeep or a hovel? No gunfire or explosions going off. *BJ's house? Yeah, BJ's house!* And he was married to her. Instantly, he felt wide-awake and aware of her body brushing against his nearly naked one as he stood in front of her. His heartbeat doubled. She was soft, sweet, oh, so feminine. "For a minute I thought I was…"

"Back on some front?" Her breasts rose and fell under her yellow sweatshirt. Small breasts, no bra. Somehow he knew. Her quick breaths streamed across his chin and neck and the temperature in the hallway seemed unbearable. She grabbed his upper arms, bringing them closer still, the contact of her skin to his like sticking his finger in an outlet.

"I have to go out. There's an emergency. You don't look so great. Are you going to be okay?"

He seriously doubted it. "Can I help you?"

"Yes, take care of yourself. Get something to eat. There's apple juice in the fridge."

"I'm fine." *If suddenly being as horny as an army marching band could be considered fine.*

How'd he get like this so fast? And why in the world did he feel that way over BJ Fairmont? Then he studied her blond hair, hanging straight to her narrow shoulders, her bright green eyes staring up at him, the dusting of freckles not hidden under makeup and her unique special scent of flowers and all things feminine, which filled his head.

This woman standing in front of him, so close he could count her eyelashes—her very long eyelashes, which framed her lovely eyes—would make a marble statue horny. "What's the emergency?"

"Ms. Millie. She might be having a stroke. Her son's with her now." She pushed at his chest, her small hands warm against his skin, turning him on even more. Her eyes dilated and she gasped. She snapped her hands back as if she'd been shocked. "Can you move, because I'm sure there's no way I can get you to do that unless you want to move, and I have to get going right now."

He gazed into her eyes, realizing her reaction had nothing to do with Ms. Millie and being a doctor and a lot to do with him nearly naked, her hands on him and the two of them so close right there in her hallway that their breaths seemed as one. She bit her bottom lip. His stomach flipped and tightened. He stepped back, but she didn't move. She deserved every inch of him and a flash of desire lit her eyes, igniting his insides.

"Oh, Flynn." She breathed the words more than said them. "You are so…damn hot." Then she threw her arms around his neck and kissed him hard, her lips sexy and seductive and surprising the living hell out of him.

He started to take her in his arms, but she pulled

away, her face flushed, her eyes glazed, her breaths fast and erratic. "Why did I do that?" She ran down the hall as if the devil himself gave chase.

He watched for a moment, mesmerized by the feel of her sweet lips on his. Then he followed, needing to be with her. "Why *did* you do that?"

He'd never asked a woman why she'd kissed him before, but this was different. This was Barbara Jean Fairmont, the last woman on earth he'd expected to kiss him now. *And he liked it a lot.*

"Where are you going?" she called over her shoulder as she snagged her black medical bag, which sat at the back door. She sounded frazzled. "Go back to sleep." She stopped and faced him. "Think of this as a dream, Flynn, or a really stupid thing on my part."

"I want to—" *to take you in my arms and kiss you back,* he thought but continued with "—do something to you." He closed his eyes for a moment, getting a grip. "I mean *for* you, not *to* you."

"You need sleep. I need sleep. *I think I need therapy!* Forget I kissed you."

She yanked open the door and went out into the cool night. He stood in the entrance, the air chilling his hot body as he watched her hurry down the path toward the gate, his heartbeat keeping time with the sound of her footfalls on the brick.

He continued to stare into the dark as she passed through the gate and rounded the house, heading for Ms. Millie's. He could still feel BJ's small hands on his bare arms, her breasts grazing his chest as she straightened against him, then her lips searing his. His insides hardened to stone and his erection pressed against his underwear. He felt like a damn high-school kid right smack in the middle of adolescence, not able to control himself after one quick kiss. Except it was a hell of a kiss.

He stepped back inside and closed the door with a thud. No need to advertise his *condition* to the whole world. Even at 0300 hours someone might be awake. *Hell, he was. Every part of him.*

All because of BJ and that one little kiss? He pictured her hair streaming out behind her, catching the moonlight. Yeah, over BJ! And thinking about her and kissing her beat the hell out of the war scenes that usually kept him from sleeping.

He headed back upstairs. What now? *Now nothing.* The simple kiss had resulted from his being nearly naked and the two of them standing close after an exhausting day. They disliked everything about each other. Then he considered her lips, her sweet body, her great eyes. Well, not everything. His present condition was an *overreaction* from not *reacting* in so long, like a parched man in a desert, gulping water.

He'd simply been in a desert. *For damn sure he'd been without.*

But the water looked so fine and tasted like pure heaven.

Sex, women? Neither had interested him…till now. Somehow, BJ Fairmont made him put aside the bad things in life and focus on the good.

Chapter Five

Morning rays slid into the kitchen as BJ shuffled her way to the sink. She caught her reflection in the half-open window. Double makeup to hide circles under her eyes hadn't worked and her hair felt bristled more than combed. She resembled a two-legged raccoon on a drinking binge more than a doctor.

She dumped coffee into the maker, then spotted the empty juice glass on the counter. *Oh, crap!* Her eyes few wide-open. She had bigger problems than needing a makeover. *She'd married Flynn MacIntire. And she'd kissed him.*

The marriage had seemed like a good idea at the time. Even during the simple ceremony, where they'd shaken hands. Then he'd moved in, run nearly naked into her in the hallway and she'd kissed him full on the mouth.

Her hands shook; her mouth went dry. Not just because she'd kissed him, but because she'd wanted more…like, tackle him to the floor, rip off his underwear, what little there was, and have sex right there on the Oriental carpet. No doubt this was due to pent-up frustration from years of imagining such a thing. But what would stop her from doing that very thing in the future?

Deep personal mortification, that was what! Maybe.

"Do you always get this little sleep?" came Flynn's deep, rich voice from the doorway. She turned slowly, praying he'd gotten just a little ugly during the night. Had grown fangs or gills or webbed fingers and feet. *Something.* But he hadn't. He looked better than ever, more rested, freshly shaven, some tangy soap scent floating her way. Thank heavens this time he had on clothes.

He walked in and leaned against the counter. "How is Ms. Millie?"

Ms Millie? Ms. Millie? Oh, yeah! Ms. Millie! "An attack of chronic stable angina."

He gave her a questioning look, and she explained. "Tightness of the chest and tingling brought on by physical or mental stress. She took one of her nitroglycerin pills, and with some rest she'll be okay. The EMS ran her into Billings for tests, just to make sure."

If BJ could get used to looking at Flynn from the neck up it might help. She wouldn't think of his firm naked chest, notice his strong forearms or the way his jeans fit just right. She thought of the fit and felt weak. She concentrated on his face to forget the rest of him, then remembered the kiss. *There was no hope!*

"Are you okay?"

Oh, Lord, no! "Tired. Coffee will help." She dumped in an extra measure and hit the On button.

Flynn pulled down two mugs from the cabinet and handed one to her, the drip of the coffee and the bird-song floating through the window the only sound. His eyes took her in, then darkened as they had last night. Her insides tied in a knot as they had last night. He swallowed; she sweated. *Oh, hell!* He said, "It was just a kiss, BJ. We've had kisses before."

Not like that. There was no *just* about it, at least for her. But he sure seemed to think so. "What kiss?"

He rolled his eyes.

"Oh, *that* kiss. We were tired. *I was tired.* It happened and it won't happen again. Hey, it's us. We have nothing to kiss about."

"We have a designated objective."

"Right, designated objective."

More coffee dripped. *Think of something to say.* "Have any idea how everyone found out about our marriage?"

Talk was good. Kept her mind off the kiss and all the rest of Flynn MacIntire.

He went to the fridge and pulled out a carton of orange juice. "You probably told someone. One of those women things. You're getting married and you want to tell your friends and talk about whatever women talk about when they're together and then they swear not to tell and they always do."

Well, there it was! Just when she needed it most, a big fat dose of chauvinist reality to snap her out of this stupid state of ogling Flynn MacIntire and his fine male attributes. All he had to do was open his mouth, instantly reminding her why the two of them would never ever get along.

She gave him a go-to-hell look. "Did it appear to you that Dixie and Maggie had any inkling at all that I was getting married?"

He shrugged dismissively. "They were hacked off you didn't include them in the plans, or you could have let it slip somewhere else."

"Women are not like that—at least, not the ones I know. A secret's a secret. You and I decided on this marriage idea late the night before, then you picked me up and we went to Billings the very next morning. No time to let anything *slip.* Though slipping a noose around your neck has definite appeal for even suggesting I can't be trusted."

"It's not so much a trust thing as a woman thing."

"A woman thing?" Her eyes bugged. "You don't get around women much, do you?"

"Been around my share. I'm trying to figure this out." He poured juice and gave her a glass. "Because it sure as hell caused us one boatload of trouble, and it would be good if it didn't cause more."

"You probably have yourself to blame, so don't go accusing me."

He cut his eyes to her.

She glared back. "I didn't tell anyone, so that leaves you. Men like to blab more than women. You went to the Cut Loose, had a few too many beers and started shooting off your mouth, and that's how news of our marriage got out."

"Not my style. Not any man's style if he's worth a damn."

"Or you told Scully or Kean and they let it out."

"Since they wanted my head on a platter for *not* telling them, that suggestion doesn't wash, either. I don't know how the hell the whole blasted town found out."

"Well, one of us has a big mouth, MacIntire." She came over to him, meeting him toe to toe. "And it ain't me, buster."

His face met hers. "Or me."

Petey and Drew suddenly appeared in the doorway, wide-eyed and afraid.

"Hi, guys," Flynn said with a smile. *At least he smiled for someone.* "What's up?"

Drew held Petey's hand tight and glanced from Flynn to BJ. "Why are you two arguing so much?"

BJ hunkered down in front of the brothers. "Flynn and I were having a discussion. We just discuss very loud."

"No, you weren't," Drew said. "You were arguing real loud. When I was little, Mommy and Daddy used to argue like that. I remember. And then Daddy left and we never saw him again. We don't want you two to do that."

When he was little? BJ felt her heart constrict. Like, Drew was so old now. BJ heard Flynn's footsteps as he approached. He bent down beside her. "How did you hear us arguing? You just came inside now and the back door is closed. And we didn't see you in the garden."

Drew shuffled his feet and Petey studied the ground.

"You were in your hideout, weren't you?" Flynn said. He pointed to the window. "Where you can hear everything in the kitchen. You heard BJ and me plan to get married."

BJ glanced back to the window. "Hideout? What hideout."

Drew shrugged and said, "Yeah, we heard you talking in the kitchen yesterday about getting married so Doc BJ can adopt a baby. We heard you arguing now, too."

BJ took their hands, one in each of hers. "Did you go to Ms. Millie's for pudding yesterday?"

All of a sudden, Petey grinned. "Yeah, Aunt Katie had to work and Ms. Millie said she'd watch us for the afternoon. She made peanut-butter pudding, the kind I can eat, and we told her about the wedding and she got all excited and started calling people on the phone and telling them the news."

He pressed his lips together and his big brown eyes rounded. "Did Drew and me do something bad?"

"Not exactly bad, but listening to people talk when they can't see you isn't very nice, especially if you tell others what you've heard."

Drew frowned. "Aunt Katie doesn't like it when Petey and me listen to her and her boyfriend. She gets all mad and pissy."

BJ cringed. "How about *upset* instead of *pissy?* And at least you realize it's not good to listen to other people's conversations. They might be discussing private things only they should know about. Good manners means you come into the room and tell people you're there and you remember to use nice words."

"Are…are you real mad at us?" Drew asked in a quiet voice. "Aunt Katie gets real mad and yells. Her boyfriend sends us to our room without TV when he doesn't want us around."

Where did this guy fit into Petey's and Drew's lives? She'd have a talk with Aunt Katie. BJ held the boys' hands tighter so they'd know she wasn't upset with them. They'd been through enough. "I have an idea. When you and Petey are in your hideout under the window I want you to tell me you're there. Can you do that for me?"

"What if we get a flag for your hideout," Flynn said. "Put it on a pole you can reach. When you're there you put up the Stars and Stripes. I'll show you how to fold it up neat and take care of it. You'll have a camp more than a hideout. How's that?"

Drew grinned at Petey and said to Flynn, "Did you have a flag at your hideout by the mine?"

"That pine tree with two trunks got in the way and we were trying to keep it a secret."

Flynn MacIntire understood little boys perfectly. Women? Completely clueless. "Go wash your hands. I'll check Petey's insulin, then make ham and eggs for breakfast."

She watched them walk down the hallway and into the bathroom. She said to Flynn. "Well, there's why Ms. Millie had her angina attack. Gossip overload. And I owe you an apology." She held out her hand.

He gripped it, his eyes dark blue and sincere, and said, "Same here."

At least, that was what she thought he'd said. Every time he touched her she wasn't sure what was going on. She let go of his hand and he picked up his juice glass. He took a long drink, the glass seemed almost lost in his grip. She stared, remembering those hands on her, holding her then shoving her behind him in protection, his body pressed against hers, hot and firm and unyielding.

She'd felt so safe…squashed, but safe all the same. If aliens or some enemy had suddenly taken over the earth, BJ Fairmont would have lived to tell the tale because Colonel Flynn MacIntire would have seen to it.

Still…this being together was never going to work. Every hunky inch of the man provided too much temptation. One day she'd get up and not care diddly about Flynn the thickheaded, arrogant, know-it-all, macho jerk she didn't like and throw herself at him, demanding feral sex on the spot from the part of him she liked a lot!

She had to get rid of him before she humiliated herself beyond all reason.

"I'll get the breakfast together, you take care of Petey," he said.

"And after breakfast we'll start on exercises and therapy to strengthen your leg. I'm sure you want to get back to the army. "

The question was—how to keep her hands off him till she got him there.

FLYNN LISTENED TO the sounds of BJ cleaning up the kitchen after breakfast as he sat at the kitchen table, studying the list of exercises she'd made up for him. Petey and Drew had chores to do at their house, then wanted to ride their bikes. Now he and BJ could get down to the business of his leg. Unfortunately, the business he thought about when he watched BJ Fairmont had nothing to do with his leg and everything to do with her hair, her eyes and her soft skin.

Being attracted to BJ one minute and wanting to wring her neck the next made no sense. And that kiss didn't help. It was high school, part two, and it was worse!

He forced himself to study the paper instead of BJ. "This isn't therapy you have outlined here—it's torture."

He slid the paper across the table. "And what's with this mineral-bath stuff?"

She put the last plate in the dishwasher, then took a magnet and affixed the list to the front of the fridge. "You could have stayed at Walter Reed. They have the best of everything—doctors, whirlpools, physical therapists. But did you? No. Since you're in Whistlers Bend, you get to go to Cabin Springs and park your butt on a rock in the middle of the hot stream."

She stopped with the dishes and slowly turned to him. Their eyes met, and he knew she was remembering Cabin Springs, just as he was.

"We didn't do anything that night."

"But we wanted to."

"It would have been a mistake. We broke up a week later. We weren't ready."

Oh, but he was so ready now, every single inch of him. *Damn, he wanted her.* But, again, it would be a mistake. Their lives didn't mesh any better now than they had then.

She added soap to the dishwasher. "I called one of your doctors. If you don't get some movement going in your leg you'll build up scar tissue and then you'll have a real problem."

He already had a real problem. A colossal problem. BJ! At the moment the only movement he could think of involved her in his arms and had nothing to do with therapy. "The short version of that conversation the two of you had is nothing's going to work so forget it?"

She faced him. "And if you believe that, you're absolutely right. And if you believe you'll get better, you're absolutely right."

"So now you're telling me I can *think* myself better? Where'd you go to medical school?"

"Attitude counts. Medicine is not an exact science. Doctors just try to—"

"Even the odds. I get it."

"I doubt it, but that's up to you." She nodded toward the hallway. "We need new X-rays."

"I've got enough of those to paper this kitchen. Use one of them." He was not stripping buck naked, with some stupid gown as his only covering, as long as BJ was around. He'd played out that scenario last night and remembered what had happened, a kiss along with a case of terminal horniness. He needed an excuse. "Are you any good at taking X-rays and reading them?"

BJ parked her hands on her hips. "Flo's sixty-seven and knows more about film than Martin Scorsese."

Flo! A harmless grandmother type would be okay. Best of all she wasn't BJ. He turned for the hall, feeling more in control; besides, he wanted to get on with therapy. He hadn't felt that way in a long time. Maybe not ever. When he'd lost his men something in him had died, too, and this last time had done him in…till now. Till BJ had walked—make that *barged*—back into his life, and suddenly her spirit and determination and focus on the living had made him feel alive, too.

The side door opened as he passed and Flo bustled in with the energy of a woman half her age. "'Morning, Flynn, you old dog."

She gave him a mischievous wink and nudged him with her shoulder. "Can't believe you landed BJ. You're not good enough for her. You realize that, don't you? Better treat her real fine or this town will hang you upside down by your privates."

She put her purse under her desk and called down the hall, "Howdy, BJ. Everyone including me is spitting mad you didn't tell us about your wedding plans. Bet you get an earful today from your patients."

Flynn rolled his eyes and BJ came down the hall. She didn't sound like a harmless grandmother. She was a woman to deal with. "This is just a marriage to help BJ adopt a baby. Agencies prefer married women."

"Sounds like an excuse to get next to BJ, if you ask me."

"Right." No reason to argue with someone who was about to see him nearly naked. He felt a little too vulnerable. He made for the X-ray room to change into his least favorite attire on earth. He closed the door, ducked behind a screen, pulled off his jeans and put on the gown. A draft chilled his bare ass; his front was no better. Between this and that *hanging* comment of Flo's, his ability to *perform* may have slipped back to its old unresponsive ways. At least, that was what he feared, till he came around the curtain and faced… "BJ?"

Blond, green eyes, beautiful even in a white lab coat. How could anyone be sexy in one of those? But damn, she was. He glanced around quick.

His breathing almost stopped along with his heart. Unfortunately, not all parts of his anatomy hit *stop*. More vital ones raced straight to *go*, and his fears of not *responding* flew right out the window. "What are you doing here?"

He ducked back behind the screen to hide his condition and craned his neck around the side.

She peered at him as if he'd lost his mind. "It's my office. I run this ship. Flo has to rearrange the schedule because we have an influx of patients to see the doctor today. Which translated means—everyone wants the scoop on our marriage, which really isn't a marriage, but no one seems to get that and they want to talk about it anyway.

"What are you doing behind that screen?"

Hiding! "Have to help Scully and Kean."

She gave him a sassy look. "They're behind the screen? Must be kind of crowded."

"They're at the lodge right now—I just remembered. I've got to go help." He ducked his head back, yanked off the gown, draped it on the chair and reached for his jeans. He'd leave his shirt untucked to hide any…bulging.

"This won't take long, Flynn," BJ countered. "We're not doing bypass surgery. It's a leg X-ray. You have on a gown. I'll keep my eyes closed."

He pulled on his shirt. "There's a big shipment of stone being delivered to the lodge. I forgot till right now."

He walked around the curtain all dressed, carrying his boots in one hand and his cane in the other to get out as fast as possible. "I don't have the time to spare. Gotta go. Bye."

She followed him down the hallway. "How will you get back into the army if you don't take time to get better? It won't happen without work. Cooperate, okay?"

If he cooperated any more, he'd shock Doc BJ's pants off! That would be okay by him, but he doubted she'd share his enthusiasm. And even if she did, then what? Fight all day, have sex all night? As good as it sounded, it was not his style, and for sure not BJ's.

"Be back later." He closed the door behind him and headed for his car, slid in and put on his boots, then made for the lodge. The stone shipment wasn't a lie, but it wasn't due till the afternoon and Scully didn't need him for that. That was the trouble. No one needed him much for anything. If he quit the army it would still function. Kean and Scully had the business and their families, and Grandma Mac had her own life.

At forty-one what did he have? A gimped leg, a bad attitude and nightmares. *"Hell!"*

BJ MARVELED AT THE EMPTY waiting room, then back to Flo behind her desk. "Okay, where'd everyone go? It's only two. Did you wave a magic wand and make them all disappear? I think we should patent that wand."

"The wand is my pen. I rescheduled for tomorrow. Maggie and Dixie called, wanting to meet you for lunch. I figured you'd better be there after the wedding episode. I'm betting they're none too happy about that."

"Try foaming at the mouth."

"Bring chocolate. They'll forgive anything if enough chocolate's involved."

BJ smiled at her nurse of fifteen years. What one didn't think of, the other did. Perfect working partners, and friends. "Thanks for saving me from my patients."

Flo sat back, pointed to the door and said in a huff. "They aren't sick, honey. They just wanted to talk about you marrying Flynn MacIntire and get all the dirt and see if you did *the deed*."

"There is no deed. As I've told everyone over and over and over, this is a—"

"Marriage of convenience." Fly waved her hand as if shooing away a fly. "Nobody wants to hear that. They want a secret love affair that involves you two not keeping your hands off each other. Everybody knows you two went together in high school and those old romances rekindled make the best stories of all. Everybody wants the dirt, the heat, the sex. They love the sex."

"There is no sex!"

"Well, ain't that a damn shame."

BJ leaned on Flo's desk, bracing herself on her arms. "We fight, Flo. Like—"

"Old married folks?"

"Like hounds over a bone. That's the way it was in high school—that's the way it is now." She stood. "If one of us says something, the other has the opposite opinion. He's a Republican. He likes Dali. He likes jazz and Hemingway and—"

"My suggestion is to forget the talking and get right to the action, the real action." Her voice got all throaty as she added, "Bet the two of you can do real well in that department and agree on everything just fine. You two got the look."

"There is no look."

"Ha!"

BJ closed her eyes, a headache threatening. "There is no action."

"You could do with some action, and I'm thinking Flynn is the perfect man for the job. Hot, sexy, virile as a bottle of Viagra."

BJ could picture Flynn just that way. Her eyes snapped open and she reached for the door handle. "I'm out of here."

Flo tipped her head. "You're running off because I'm right about you and Flynn, and you're afraid to hear it because it might give you ideas."

BJ stopped and said, "I'm forty. I'm not afraid, I do not run."

"Honey, I don't care how old you are. You are so afraid you don't know which end's up, and I'm here to tell you it doesn't matter, as long as one's up and one's down."

Flo laughed and BJ slapped her palm to her forehead, trying to ignore the instant heat spreading to every inch of her body as a mental image of the *up-and-down* situation flashed before her. She ran out the door with more of Flo's laughter ringing in her ears. BJ called over her shoulder, "I'll be back for evening appointments."

Maybe, she thought as she made her way to the Purple Sage, *if she survived the rest of the day.* Everyone seemed to think that since she was the town doctor and

Flynn was the town hero and they'd had a brief town romance, their business was public domain and everyone had claims on it.

She wondered if Flynn encountered the same harassment as she did. She considered his fierce army-colonel expression. No one in his right mind would harass Flynn MacIntire...except her, of course. Then again, when it came to Flynn she'd never been in her right mind.

She rounded the corner and spied the Murphy twins rushing her way from across the street. *Oh, no, the biggest gossips in town, next to Ms. Millie.* They'd pump BJ for information, and she was not in the mood. She started to duck into the hardware store, till she spotted two of her mother's friends inside, who also spotted her.

Trapped! She'd have to run for it, or at least walk fast, since running wasn't exactly her thing. She lowered her head and walked as fast as possible to the Purple Sage. No one would follow her there—too noisy with lunchtime clatter for a proper inquisition. BJ saw Maggie and Dixie at their usual table by the window, neither looked too friendly.

Most times BJ ignored the gooey treats under the glass dome on the counter, but this was a gooey-treat situation. She ordered three pieces of peanut-butter pie. Balancing them she sidestepped other customers, pretending not to hear their questions about her marriage and Flynn. She said to Maggie and Dixie, "I bring gifts of great joy."

They continued to stir their coffee.

The silent treatment. "Okay." BJ shrugged, almost

losing the plates. "I'll just take these to the three cow-boys in the corner booth. I bet they—"

"Don't even think about giving that pie away," Dixie ordered, grabbing one of the pieces from BJ's hand. "I love peanut-butter pie."

"Really? I didn't know that." BJ placed the other piece in front of Maggie, who said, "But I shouldn't eat this, or I'll never fit into my wedding suit. I'll look like a big pink sausage."

BJ pulled out a chair and put her own piece on the table. She said to Maggie, "You could drop it off at the sheriff's office for Jack. I bet he'd appreciate peanut-butter pie."

Maggie nodded. "Maybe I better taste it first to make sure it's okay."

BJ handed her a fork. "Wouldn't want our sheriff to get sick. That would be terrible."

"Just awful," Maggie said around a mouthful. Her eyes misted and an expression of pure rapture covered her face at first bite. "Why," she said on a sigh, "is it that all the stuff in life we like most is so bad for us? A carrot never tastes like this."

"I have a theory," Dixie ventured. "If you eat the car-rot first you still want the pie. But if you eat the pie first you don't want the carrot. So why not just skip the car-rot and go right for the pie? Saves time."

BJ bit back a laugh. "Like cutting out the middle-man."

"My point exactly." Dixie forked another bite. "Speaking about *the man,* how's yours?"

"Mine?" BJ looked from Maggie to Dixie. "You got

me over here to pump me for information about Flynn and me?"

Maggie tsked. "Well, of course. You owe us. Give."

"There's nothing to give." BJ ran her hand over her face. "I should get a tape recording of this so I don't have to keep saying it over and over. There is no man in my life, just Flynn and—"

"He is all *man* and then some," Dixie said, fork raised in declaration. "And if you don't see that, you are in serious trouble."

"But he's not *in* my life."

"Why not?" Maggie claimed another bite and wiggled her eyebrows. "He's under your roof. You eat together, talk together and—" she grinned hugely "—why wouldn't you sleep—"

"We sleep in separate rooms," BJ finished.

"That's it? There's nothing more to tell?" Dixie asked. "You should be ashamed."

"We didn't do anything."

Maggie snagged BJ's pie. "Well, that's darn disappointing. I'd hoped for better, much better. You can go now. We're all through here."

"What do you mean, I can go? You asked me to come. I brought pie."

Dixie licked a spot of peanut butter from her fork. "Since you have nothing good to share and we already got the pie, you can go."

"We're still not talking to you," Maggie added.

"I don't believe this," BJ seethed. "You just wanted gossip?"

Maggie nodded. "Yep, that pretty much covers it. We

asked you here because we were dying of curiosity, and now we see there's nothing to be curious about. And since we're still mad at you, leave."

BJ sat back in her chair. "Maybe I'm lying. Maybe MacIntire and I have had incredible sex in every room of the house and in every position known to the human race?"

"You wouldn't be calling him *MacIntire* without turning red or stammering," Dixie said. "You're not a loose woman. The wild sex would get to you and we'd see that there'd been hanky-panky."

Dixie turned to Maggie. "I can't believe there's been no hanky-panky." She waved at BJ dismissively.

BJ stood. "Remind me again why we're best friends?"

Maggie shrugged. "I'll think of something as soon as I finish this pie."

"I thought best friends forgave all."

Maggie huffed and offered BJ a beady-eyed stare. "Except being excluded from a certain *wedding*. That's going to take some time."

BJ stormed for the door, yanked it open. All this abuse for a baby?

Labor pains, that was what this was. Natural mothers had contractions to have a baby; she had Maggie, Dixie, Mother and the whole blasted town of Whistlers Bend to deal with. And she had Flynn MacIntire, the biggest pain of all, living with her. Not because they fought, but because of the other times, like when they were alone and didn't fight and she got all hot and bothered looking at him and felt certain the minute he did open his mouth they'd have war.

How could she deal with both sides of Flynn?

Chapter Six

Flynn drove away from the lodge. The day seemed a longer one than usual, maybe because Scully was home recuperating and not on the job. He should go to Cabin Springs, soak and then do some of those stretching exercises to get his leg moving better. He turned the car onto the road that led there. A cloud of dust went with him, enveloping the car, and he suddenly remembered another road just like it on the other side of the globe, when he'd been driving in a convoy and his whole world had blown apart.

He stopped, stared off into space, the horror replaying again and again and again in his brain. Sweat drenched his clothes, his hands shook, and he squeezed his eyes shut against the memory. Then the peaceful Pryor Mountains reappeared and the serenity of Whistlers Bend surrounded him.

He rested his head against the steering wheel, drawing in ragged breaths. How could he get past this? It wasn't the first time he'd been in combat; he'd spent most of his life there. Maybe that was the problem, like the drop of water that falls into a bucket when there isn't enough room for even one more drop.

He needed to go on. He needed to function, but he had no idea how to do it. Doctors had tried to help him, but the decision was really all his.

He did a U-ee and drove back down the dusty road, any enthusiasm for soaking and exercise gone. Not that he'd had all that much enthusiasm before. He turned onto the two-lane as a box truck flew around from the other direction, followed by two more. Flynn swerved to the side, sliding on the gravel, dodging a collision by a hair.

"What the hell!" He fought to control the car. What was a box truck doing here? Any truck other than the cattle variety never came this way. He glanced in the rearview mirror, the clouds of dust obliterating any chance of his catching the license plate.

The drivers were lost? Except they had to realize they'd left the main road five miles back. And why were they heading toward the old depot? It was a nothing place miles from nowhere.

He drove back to town, parked in front of the sheriff's office, got his cane and went inside. Jack Dawson glanced up, then leaned back in his chair, cop face firmly in place. Once a Chicago cop, always a Chicago cop, "Flynn MacIntire, what can I do for you?"

Flynn held out his hand. "Accept my apology for being a horse's ass the other night."

Jack laughed. "Been a horse's ass on more than one occasion myself." He stood and took Flynn's hand. "No harm done. Congratulations on getting hitched. Got to admit, I never saw that one coming."

"Hell, neither did I." Flynn gave a lopsided grin and sat down. Jack parked on the edge of his desk and Flynn continued. "Have you heard anything about box trucks running up by Silver Gulch?"

Jack didn't say anything, but the glint of interest in his eyes gave him away. Flynn went on. "Spotted three of them about twenty minutes ago."

"Any markings? License plates?"

"Plain white. Too busy staying on the road to catch the plates. Thought about giving chase but didn't want to step on any toes in case you had something in place."

Jack raked a hand through his hair. "Trucks come and go at random times and at different places in the area. Best we can tell, they're meeting up, offloading whatever and fading away, using back roads. Something's up and it's not legal, or they'd meet in town. These guys are impossible to catch with just Roy and me to cover so much territory, and alerting the good citizens could wind up in a shoot-out over nothing."

"Thought I'd mention it. If I can help, just say the word."

"I might do that. Keep this to yourself. We don't want to tip our hand."

Flynn nodded and stood and Jack walked him to the door. "I suppose we'll be seeing you and BJ at the reception tomorrow night at the country club."

Flynn stopped dead. "Ah, hell, I forgot about that."

"Your mother-in-law sure hasn't. Her daughter's a class act, but Margaret can be a handful." Jack patted Flynn on the back. "Good luck, Colonel. You're going to need it."

Flynn drove to the next block, stopped in front of

BJ's house, now his house, and went inside. Flo hurried down the hall. "'Evening, Colonel. Have a good day? BJ's just finishing up."

BJ stuck her head out of an examining room. "How'd the soaking go?"

"It didn't."

Her brow furrowed and she met up with him in the hallway. "We need to talk."

He leaned against the wall, tucking the hook of his cane into his front jeans pocket. "It's never good when a woman says that. It means she's going to tell you something you don't want to hear. Right now I want to hear about a beer and a cigarette."

"Oh, that's going to do you a lot of good. The cancer-stick prescription for good health?"

He headed for the stairs, for a shower. BJ trailed behind. "You're not going to improve if you don't follow any of my suggestions."

He halted at the foot of the stairs and faced her. "And I'm probably not going to improve, period, so what's the point?"

"You getting better is part of the deal."

"Screw the deal."

Flo stomped down the hall and with a flourish pulled open the front door. She bowed, gesturing toward the outside like a flamboyant doorman—or doorwoman, in this case. "*There.* Now you have the whole blessed town as an audience for your infernal bickering," she said. "Anyone who thought your marriage was a match made in heaven now knows they're dead wrong. I've never met two more mismatched, pigheaded, uncompromising people in all my born days. No better now than twenty years ago. It's the wrong marriage for all the right reasons.

"So how are you going to make it work?"

"Hell if I know." Flynn grabbed his cane and stepped around BJ and took the stairs. He went for the shower, turned it full-blast hot and stripped off his clothes. Flo was right. He and BJ had to make this marriage work, at least for a while. Not because of his leg, but because some kid out there deserved it.

He and BJ needed to set some guidelines. Something that would keep them apart but allow them to live together. The heated looks, heated thoughts, along with the heated words, were driving him nuts. This love-hate relationship they'd gotten themselves into sucked and had to get straightened out.

He dried off with one of BJ's minuscule rose towels, dressed in clean clothes and went back downstairs. Flo was gone; BJ was finishing up with the last patient of the day. Evening had fallen, casting long shadows across the waiting room and into the hall. He dropped down into the leather couch to wait for her and closed his eyes, fatigue washing over him like some giant wave.

He listened to the steady rise and fall of BJ's soothing, patient voice; the tick of the clock in the hallway that got louder, then louder, faster, then faster; the hum of an engine…a convoy on an unpaved road. Explosions, gunfire, someone shoving him. *He could save them this time.* This time it would be okay. He reached out and grabbed the soldier, throwing him hard to the ground, covering him with his body for protection. It worked; he'd won.

Except it wasn't the enemy at all. It was BJ. He had her pinned to the floor. She appeared dazed but okay. He dropped his head beside hers. "Damn."

BJ FELT FLYNN'S BREATHS hot and fast on her neck, his heart beating wild. She had no idea what to do. Yelling *snap out of it* seemed a bit harsh, considering he'd been in the throes of some sort of nightmare when she'd woken him. Besides, having Flynn on top of her was something she'd dreamed of a hundred times. Pity it had taken a nightmare to get him here. But right now she had something more important to consider. Flynn needed her and she had no idea what to do.

She couldn't come up with a single class or article or symposium that applied to this situation. She went with female gut instinct, framed his face between her palms and brought it up to hers. She kissed him.

Not a sexy kind of kiss like last night's, but a reassuring kind from someone who cared. No matter how much they argued, she did care. She always would. His lips were hard, unmoving, unresponsive as she gently, slowly, planted kisses across his top lip, then bottom, working her way from one corner to the other. Gradually, his mouth softened, his body relaxed, melting into hers. His mouth moved, then formed to hers and he returned one kiss, then another.

He took his head away, and the heated look in his eyes said he wasn't thinking army. She kissed him again. "I was worried about you. This wasn't a come-on."

"I understand." He didn't budge. His eyes darkened

to rich velvet and he brushed her hair from her cheek and her forehead. "But this is," he said with a definite ring of command. "One minute we want to strangle each other, the next minute this."

He kissed *her.* Hot, possessive, sensual, urgent and more wonderful than her wildest dreams.

His rugged, unyielding strength surrounded her. She wrapped her arms around his neck, her fingers sliding across his broad shoulders, then bunching into the material of his shirt as she brought him close, not quite believing she was really with him.

His tongue engaged hers in an erotic dance, suggesting exactly what he wanted. He dropped quick hot kisses across her chin, making her quiver, then stopping where her blouse closed in a vee.

He pushed himself to a kneeling position, one leg on either side of her, trapping her. Holy Toledo. She'd dreamed about this and here she was.

He yanked his shirt over his head and threw it onto the couch. Her gaze snapped away from the zipper and focused on his naked chest, his torso rising and falling with rapid, barely controlled breathing. "Are you expecting more patients?"

"I have no patience, Flynn. I want you now."

He grinned. "*Patients* as in doctor and patients."

"Door's locked." She reached for his belt buckle, but his hands stopped hers. "Are you sure about this?"

"Flynn, I locked it myself. It's a dead bolt."

His eyes brightened; an enticing smile softened his lips. "I mean, are you sure about *this*." He trailed one firm finger down her middle, to her waistband.

She felt light-headed, woozy. She swallowed. "I've wanted this for twenty years."

Her eyes widened. So did his. She froze. Did she just say what she thought she said? What would he do? Laugh, snicker, lord it over her?

"Twenty years?"

"On and off."

"You never said anything."

"Maybe I should have interjected *I want to have sex with you* between our battles."

"It sure as hell would have gotten my attention." He took her mouth in a searing kiss that shocked her and drove all doubt right out of her brain that he wanted her as much as she wanted him. His demanding tongue took possession of hers and his left hand tangled into her hair as he cupped the back of her head possessively while his other hand held him upright.

Her pulse drummed; her insides clenched. She touched his muscled chest, the sprinkle of soft curls against her palms exciting her. *Like she needed more of that!* Her fingers traced the smooth skin of his abs, firm from years of military training. Her thumb skimmed down his middle, and paused at his belt buckle. Then she undid it, unsnapped his jeans and fondled him.

Flynn broke the kiss and closed his eyes, his body suddenly rigid. That she had this effect on him set her on fire.

"Oh, BJ." He righted, his eyes bright with arousal now. He unbuttoned her blouse. Worshipfully, he spread the sides of the blouse and traced the curve of her cleavage with his fingertips. Her breasts swelled and strained against her bra in anticipation of his touch. She couldn't take in enough air. Her lungs burned; her body grew heavy with wanting him.

"What you do to me is incredible," Flynn said in a husky whisper. "Your skin, your scent, your heat, the way you respond to me. I want you bad." Then he lowered his head and took her left nipple into his mouth, material and all.

Yikes! Her body arched, the nub in his now-wet mouth hardening as his tongue suckled her. She needed to touch him without any barriers. She dragged his briefs lower and her hands stroked his ridged flesh.

"BJ," he murmured against her flesh, "you're incredible. *You're heaven.*"

"You're huge."

He grinned, then chuckled. "It's been a while for me."

"And you think the spinster town doctor gets much action?"

"You're no spinster. You're hot!" He slid his hand to her back and undid her bra. "We need to make up for lost time." He sat up and peeled her bra over her breasts, then let out a long breath saying, "You're gorgeous."

"Barely B," she lied. "You *have* been without for a while."

"You're perfect." He bent his head and kissed her left breast, then the right. She massaged his erection again, loving the throb of him in her hands. She reached lower and cupped his full firm testicles; his body quivered in response.

His fingers found her zipper and her slacks loosened. He sat up, his breathing fast and shallow. "We have a problem."

"Flynn, we have so many. Do we have to discuss another one *now?*"

"Birth control? You said you were too old for a baby."

"Luteal phase defect."

"That is code for…?"

"Low progesterone levels. You aren't my first lover. No babies without artificial insemination."

He gave her a roguish grin. "Doc, there sure as hell isn't anything artificial going on tonight." He hooked his fingers in her slacks and panties and glided them down over her hips, her thighs, her knees and calves to her ankles.

He took off her shoes and tossed one over his left shoulder. It landed somewhere with a thump. Then he tossed the other over his right shoulder. He removed her pants, leaving her naked from waist to toes. Good thing she was lying down, because the hot look in his eyes turned her legs to jelly. He stood. Keeping his eyes fixed on her, he slid off his jeans.

She appreciated every wonderful, fully aroused inch of him. He said, "You are so lovely."

"So are you."

He knelt, but instead of covering her with himself, he spread her legs and planted a wet kiss on the inside of her left knee.

Her eyes met his over her torso. "What are you doing?"

His left eyebrow arched. "Fulfilling a dream."

"*This* wasn't part of the dream."

His eyes went smokey-blue. This time a devil grin parted his lips. "Liar."

Then he planted a row of hot kisses along the inside of one thigh, then the other. She felt embarrassed and tried to close her legs, but he held firm. The smell of sex filled the room as his fingers, his tongue, his lips trailed *up*, closer, more intimately, making her tremble with excitement and expectation. "Flynn, is this the way middle-aged women…act?"

She heard him laugh, then she felt his mouth on her moist most sensitive flesh. Her insides quivered, tightened and flamed as an uncontrollable orgasm shook her body. "Oh, Flynn!"

"Just let it happen, BJ."

Pure heaven rolled over her again and again, proving middle-aged women did *this* so very well. In fact, she hadn't done it this well as a young woman. Forty was…good. Great. She should have turned forty a long time ago. And then she felt his hard body on hers, his knees spreading her legs wider still, his arousal pressing into her softness, opening her and then filling her with himself.

She dug her fingers into his shoulders, her hips arching, meeting him. He thrust into her, building her up again—*could she really do this again?* His lovemaking completed every dream, every fantasy, she'd ever had about Flynn MacIntire.

Rapture spiraled through her. Her moans, raw with emotion, echoed through the room. She tightened her thighs around his middle, drawing their bodies closer still, sending her and him into a climax. Nothing could have prepared her for this, *for Flynn.*

FLYNN FELT THE WORLD explode around him, and this time it had nothing to do with bombs and mortars and gunfire, and everything to do with Barbara Jean Fairmont and incredible, mind-blowing, heart-stopping sex. If he had known it would be this terrific he'd have dreamed of it for twenty years, too!

He rested his forehead against hers, keeping his weight from her. She wasn't that much shorter, but he had her by sixty pounds. Squashing her flat didn't seem like an appropriate thank-you for great sex.

And that was all it was. That was all it could be. A life of great sex wouldn't compensate for a life of arguing. He opened his eyes; hers were still closed. Her chest rose and fell with ragged breaths, returning to normal. Her breasts were still full and round with passion, nipples hard and pink from their lovemaking. "You're incredible," he said in a voice not very steady at all.

Her eyes opened and met his. She licked her sexy lips, soft and red. Her green eyes sparkled with satisfaction. "You're the one who's incredible."

"Satisfy any dreams?"

She smiled. "You have no idea."

"Maybe I do." He didn't move but drank her in. He didn't want this to end, and he knew the real world waited for them with more problems than he wanted to face. She stroked his cheek, then slowly ran her fingers over his lips, chin and throat, her touch warm and gentle and caring. Her eyes darkened. "Can we just stay here for maybe the next twenty years? Since we took twenty years to get here, it only seems fitting."

"And we do fit." He kissed her, memorizing the feel of her lips on his. "Oh, Doc, I wish we could stay here."

He rolled from her and sat up, then helped her up beside him. "What now?" she asked.

He swiped his hand over his face. "Now we redefine the objective and design strategy."

"We're not storming the citadel, Flynn. We're trying to live together without homicide." Her eyes met his and she let out a resigned sigh. "Which has a lot of similarities to storming the citadel."

She raked her silky hair back from her face and looked at him. "I need food."

"Sex gives you an appetite?"

She pursed her lips. "Since you know everything else about me—" she blushed, making her all the more attractive "—it's been so long, I don't remember if it does or not."

He laughed and stood, then reached down to help her up, taken by the fact of how willowy she was. He pulled her into his arms and kissed her, reveling in her naked body next to his. "You haven't forgotten a thing, Doc."

This time she laughed, the contagious sound suddenly mixing with the ringing phone. She closed her eyes. "Back to the real world."

She turned away and sprinted from the room, her sleek frame silhouetted by the faint glow of moonlight slipping through the window. He pulled on his briefs and jeans, listening to BJ's voice in the distance. The floorboard creaked as she made her way back to him. She got her panties and slacks from the floor, saying, "Baby Deters has a nasty cough, and firsttime parents

Mommy and Daddy Deters are frantic." She shrugged into her clothes. "We can strategize as soon as I get back." She buttoned her blouse. "Have you seen my other shoe?"

He held it up in triumph. "Think I liked it better when I took it off. I'll cook up some dinner."

Even in the dim light he saw her head snap up in surprise. "You cook?"

"Can you change a tire on your car?"

She shrugged. "Of course."

"Guess we've crossed those gender barriers." He held up her other shoe and she snagged it. She hopped down the hall, slipping it on as she went, then pulled her medical bag from behind Flo's desk.

He opened the door for BJ and she paused in the entrance, the moon at her back. She trailed her hand over his chest to his arm and paused at the tank tattooed on his biceps. She kissed it, then looked up at him, her eyes clouded. "I don't know what's going to happen from here on out, Colonel MacIntire, but as for the twenty-year wait— she winked "—it was worth it."

She left and quietly closed the door behind her. He stared at it for a while. Twenty years was a hell of a long time to wait for anything, but on this one thing they agreed—it had been worth the wait. The question was…what the hell would they do about it now that the waiting was over?

BJ CHECKED HER WATCH as she trudged up the garden path. Ten o'clock. She'd spent two hours treating the sniffles—the baby hadn't even had a full-blown cold.

Then again, better to have overconcerned parents than a guardian who didn't want to be bothered. Tomorrow she'd pay another visit to the Deterses to make sure they were okay, and she'd visit Aunt Katie again and check on things there. Kids, job, diabetes, dating. What a combination.

When she opened the side door, wonderful food smells washed over her. Her mouth watered and her stomach growled. She followed her nose to the kitchen and the homey clatter of pots, pans sizzling and…jazz? She hated jazz. To her it sounded like a radio on two stations at once. She stopped in the doorway and Flynn caught sight of her. "Hey. Hungry?"

Chicken, potatoes, garlic bread, green beans. "You… fried? You carbed? You buttered?"

She couldn't remember the last time she'd fried anything except an egg for the boys.

He pointed to the stove. "And I vegetabled. Is that bad?"

Not if you're a soldier and you sweated your butt off in the field all day. But for a sedentary doctor… She should just get a glue gun and slap all that food on her butt right now, because it would end up there eventually. Flynn had worked really hard, so she went with a big smile and said, "Smells great!"

He heaped her plate with enough food to last a week, then did the same to his and sat across from her. He dug in. "You know," he said around a bit of fried chicken, "I thought about identifying the objective, and decided that was us getting along, right?"

She bit into the chicken. "This is really good." And

she meant it. How long had it been since she'd had any fried meat? Years! She felt her arteries constrict.

"Well," he continued, "I figured if I took one bedroom and the guest bath, *put* my stuff there and made it livable, that would work."

"Livable?"

"I already moved the picture and some of the furniture into the attic and tomorrow I'll—"

She stopped mid chew, hoping food didn't dangle from her mouth. She stared at him across the table.

His eyes met hers. "I moved some of your more *feminine* accoutrements—"

"My what?" Her eyes bugged.

His eyes narrowed. "Trappings, frills, bits and pieces of female paraphernalia. I can't live surrounded with all that...stuff."

She put down her fork. "Stuff—give me some examples."

"Towels, lotions, shampoos, spongy things, hair dryer. That kind of junk."

"That kind of junk is Christian Dior and costs the earth." She leaned across the table and waved her fork, complete with piece of chicken, at him. "Shouldn't you have discussed this strategy with me? We could have come up with a solution together?" *Like you moving to the Holiday Inn in Billings.*

"You were busy. I took care of it. Done." He sank his teeth into a drumstick, looking more caveman than houseguest.

"But this is my place."

"And mine—at least, for a while."

She chomped the chicken off the fork, amazed she didn't chip a tooth in the process, then hacked off another chunk so she wouldn't be tempted to turn her utensils into lethal weapons, draw and quarter Flynn MacIntire on the spot and hang his sorry carcass out the window. Then she remembered his carcass and her mouth went dry. She remembered that carcass in action, and suddenly, she couldn't breathe.

Then she considered her house. *The vultures could have him.* "Couldn't you have just pitched a tent behind the compost pile or something?"

He glared.

"All right, all right. That's a little extreme." She jabbed some green beans. "Maybe it isn't as bad as it sounds." She brightened. "I'm tired, overreacting. I'm sure it's fine. Just make yourself at home."

"I have."

Why did those two words sound so ominous? She bit into the bread and tore off a chunk with her teeth.

"It looks pretty good."

She wouldn't ask him to define *good.* "Butter?" She held up the bread. "I don't have butter here. Did you shop?"

"Picked it up from Grandma Mac when I went over for my jazz collection."

Jazz! She put down her fork; her stomach rolled.

"That's all you're going to eat? I have dessert. Picked up a pie at the Purple Sage. Dixie and I got talking and she gave me some denim curtains. Used to be in her son's room."

BJ's eyes widened to cover half her face, and her jaw

dropped. "D-denim? You changed my custom-made Waverly curtains for...*denim?*"

"They're terrific. And green instead of blue. No navy." He leaned across the table. "And they don't have flowers."

"You *like* flowers."

"About as much as you like fried food. In small doses." He nodded at her plate. "Dixie lent me the matching bedspread to the curtains. That should make you happy. Everything will match."

"To what? A barracks?" She leaned across the table, her nose nearly touching his. She remembered the last time they'd been like this, nose to nose, having terrific sex. Now they were arguing...just like old times. "The comforter on that bed is from Neiman Marcus. It's Siberian goose down, the epitome of comfort and relaxation."

"And it's covered with some big red flowers, and now it's in the attic."

She pushed her chair back, stood and peered down at him. She considered wringing his neck but counted to ten, then stomped down the hall. She climbed the stairs, turned left and looked into his room. Green denim.

Oh, Lord, olive-colored things are in my house, and not just on the plants.

She heard him come up the steps and felt him behind her, his breath light on her neck, making her tingly— or maybe that feeling was a bad reaction over this room.

"Great, huh. I knew once you saw it, it would be okay."

The worst part was he was serious! "You should mount an Uzi over your headboard. Complete the ambience. Maybe park a tank in the backyard."

"We don't use Uzis in the army and a Big Boy wouldn't fit in the backyard."

He winked. She turned from the bedroom from hell—though hell would have more flash—and went across the hall to the bathroom. "Where's my shower curtain? Where'd this tan plastic thing come from? Where are my towels?"

"You mean those skimpy things about the size of a postage stamp that wouldn't cover my…" They exchanged looks. "Never mind."

She spread her hands wide, taking in the white-tiled bathroom and getting her mind back to the moment. "I can't live like this. These towels are brown."

"They match the shower curtain."

"They're nearly threadbare, and they're hanging in my bathroom."

"I've had them for about ten years, taken them with me all over the world."

She pulled one off the rack and held it up to him. "Redeem them in for frequent-flier miles, *but don't hang them in my bathroom.*"

He pulled himself up tall. She did the same. "Till I get back in the army," he said, "and I mean really back in, this is my bathroom. I can't move out. Your mother and my grandmother will go ape-shit if I do, and you have to admit that's worse than a little denim and some brown towels, and I *know* it's worse than flowers. We can't get a divorce or all that baby stuff you ordered will go to waste because the adoption will be down the tubes."

He hitched his thumb over his shoulder. "So, this is it, Doc. Deal."

Chapter Seven

"Deal? With this?" BJ huffed and planted her hands on her hips. "How do I do that?"

"I'm not a permanent fixture here, just passing through. When I'm gone you can have all your flowers and prissy little things back. It's just a room."

"Two rooms, counting the bath. Welcome to the home of Bunker Bob." She spun on her heel and headed back downstairs.

"Where are you going?" he called over the railing.

"To clean up the kitchen."

"I can do that."

"You cooked. I'll clean. Why don't you soak in *your* new bathroom. *Headfirst!*"

She had to get away from him before there was a homicide in Whistlers Bend. *MacIntire's!* Her twenty-year fantasy of wanting Flynn, kissing him, making love to him, had come true, then ended with a crash. Once again she and MacIntire were at each other's throats. Everything was back to normal.

How could she be madder at him than ever before

and be hotter for him than ever before? Then she considered the waiting room and the two of them there. She had her answer. Lust didn't need to make sense; it just was. But it wasn't all lust. Flynn did have his good points. He'd married her to help her adopt, Petey and Drew worshipped him, and the man was a true hero.

She opened the pantry. She needed comfort food, dealing with Flynn food. *She needed a fix.* She reached behind the cylinder of oatmeal, the jar of honey, the two boxes of dried milk and connected with the brown paper bag stashed in the corner. She sat at the table, fished out the contents, tore off the cellophane and popped a chicken into her mouth. *Thank the sugar gods for Peeps.* Nothing like marshmallows covered in sugar for inspiration.

"What the hell are you doing?"

She swung around, a purple chicken's butt hanging out of her mouth. She poked it all the way in with her index finger as Flynn entered. He picked up the package. "You're eating this and you give me grief about fried and buttered and carbed?"

"And smoking," she added around a gooey mouthful. She pinked as he started to clear the dishes, could feel the heat rushing to her cheeks. "Can't help it," she mumbled as he packed glasses and utensils in the dishwasher.

"And you can't tell anyone," she continued after she'd swallowed. Gulping Peeps was a sin. They were to be savored. "I'm the official hawker of healthy eating around here, and if it gets out I eat sugar-covered marshmallows no one in Whistlers Bend will ever listen to me again."

She wiped the counter as he did the table. "I had to drive all the way to Billings at Easter to get these so no one would see me. Besides, it's against the law for a husband to rat out his wife. I think it's in the Constitution or something."

He eyed her. "Or something. Life is never boring with you, Doc, I'll give you that."

"I've never come home and found that the Decorating Diva of the First Brigade had taken over my house."

"Two rooms," he called over his shoulder as he walked down the hall. He stopped and she heard him turn back toward her.

"Now you're back to redo my kitchen into a mess hall?"

"How'd you know I was with the First Brigade? You're not exactly into the army thing."

"Good grief, MacIntire. You're all over the newspapers. Everybody knows. Two Silver Stars, a Purple Heart. Commendations out the ying-yang."

"Nobody remembers that kind of thing."

"Of course they do. I remember."

He gave her a long look. "Yeah, you do. More than I ever thought you would." He retraced his steps and she heard the stairs creak as he went to his bunker. She didn't understand what that last crack was about, but it didn't matter. He'd made plans for her house. Now she'd make plans for him and how to get him out of her life.

And as the pearl-gray of dawn broke over the mountains, inching its way into her room, she decided to put her plan into action. Not just because of the great remodeling fiasco but because sleeping—or more accurately, *not sleeping*—next to Flynn's room and not *in* Flynn's room drove her nuts.

She pulled on mauve sweatpants with matching top, grabbed two pillows from her bed and made her way toward the bunker for a direct assault. The door was ajar and she went inside, stood at the back of the room and threw one pillow, which missed the bed entirely in typical uncoordinated BJ Fairmont style. She prayed for better luck, thought how Tiger Woods got that ball into that little cup, aimed again, then hurled the second pillow. Miracle of miracles, it landed squarely on Flynn's head.

Flynn bolted upright, ready to tackle the world. His eyes cleared and focused on her. "What are you doing, Fairmont?"

"Staying out of harm's way. I remember the last time I woke you."

He ran his hand over his bare head. "And you woke me because…?"

"You're getting up in a half hour anyway to go to work, and I want to massage your leg and get you going on your exercises. You have to get out of here before we kill each other."

He studied her through the dim light. A slow smile spread across his face. "Let's massage something else."

"I'm serious, Flynn."

"So am I, Doc." His look turned roguish. A sudden bulge under the thin sheet confirmed his words.

She put her hands to her hips. "You still want sex with me, even though we agree on nothing?"

He shrugged his broad, bare shoulders. "Okay."

She hadn't counted on the sheet settling around his waist and the broad bare part. She'd only counted on the *get rid of Flynn* part.

"Do you always think with the lower part of your anatomy early in the morning?"

"I'm a guy. It happens."

"Well, this can happen, too." She moved closer, concentrating on his thick head and not his nakedness. "I'm massaging your leg, then we're going for walk around the block without your cane."

He gazed at her for a long moment, a faraway expression in his eyes. "No way, Doc. It's not a walking-without-the-cane kind of day."

"And just what kind of day would it take for you to agree to that?"

"A distant one." He lay back down. "Go away. My leg, my problem. Besides, I've got that flag for Drew and Petey. I need to attach a pole to the house."

"It's *our* problem. You're living in *my* house and we'll be back in plenty of time for Drew and Petey, and what are you doing to my house now?"

"Putting up a flagpole. A short one. Remember my idea? Ya know, you're getting to be a nag."

"And you're an interloper." She left the room, because if she didn't, she'd jump into bed with him.

She got out of the house and made for the Purple Sage. With luck, Dixie had the early shift. BJ wanted coffee and she had to bean Dixie over the head for all her great help to Flynn. Denim! Dixie knew she hated denim. It fell in the same category as blah-brown. Had she ever worn any of those colors in her entire life?

She pushed open the café door and zeroed in on her best friend, who was serving up ham and eggs, along with a good dose of flirting, to the hardworking cowboys. Maggie plopped down at their table, looking like something the cat had coughed up.

BJ plucked a feather from Maggie's hair. "What the heck happened to you? I keep seeing you in town earlier and earlier. Maybe you should move in from Sky Notch."

"Do I have to hear insults this time of day, especially from someone in mauve and clean Nikes? But if you need answers, Andy happened, again. Seems to be having a real good time of this." She gulped coffee. "Every time I get close he laughs and trots his one-ton girth off in the opposite direction, knowing I can't do one darn thing about it."

BJ sipped the coffee Dixie had poured. "Your buffalo laughs? How much sleep did you get last night? Maybe you should persuade someone to help you round up Andy."

"Dan Pruitt goes with me sometimes, but if Andy won't come to me, he won't come to anybody. Last night he scared the bejeebers out of some kids camping down by the lake, plowed through Denis Turpin's chicken coop. I helped Denis chase prize pullets till dawn. There are enough feathers in my car to make my own pillow."

"What are you doing here so early?" Dixie asked BJ. "Don't you and Flynn have better things to do at this hour?" Dixie asked.

"I tried to get him to exercise, but he wouldn't cooperate."

Dixie's eyebrows arched. "Can't believe a guy like Flynn MacIntire would turn down morning exercise. Doesn't seem the type at all."

BJ threw her hands in the air. "I mean exercise as in real exercise. Did I say anything, one single word, about *sex?*"

Everyone in the café stopped dead and stared her way. Okay, this had gone on long enough. She stood, held on to Dixie's shoulder for support and stepped on the chair. "Listen up, everybody. Flynn and I are doing this marriage thing so I can adopt a baby and help Flynn with his leg. That's all there is to it, not one thing more. Get the picture? Now you all don't have to get ear strain listening to our conversation over here."

She stepped down and reclaimed her seat. "There." She dusted her hands together. "That should put an end to the gossip. And why are you two suddenly all chummy with me? Thought we had *issues.*"

Dixie sat across from BJ and put her coffee carafe on the table. "First, no one believed a word you just said. You made too big a deal out of it and you called Flynn Flynn, not MacIntire. You always call him Mac-Intire, so something's changed, and I'm guessing that exercise you didn't do this morning already happened last night and—" she rushed on "—the reason Maggie and I are chummy is your mother's having your reception tonight at the Rocky Fork Country Club and we don't want you to uninvite us."

"I suck at affairs."

Dixie stood. "It's not an affair. You're married. Get used to it."

"I could never get used to being married to MacIntire. And I should uninvite you after you sold me down the river with that denim thing."

Dixie sauntered toward a cowboy needing a coffee refill. "Flynn's as handsome as all get out and has a killer smile. I'm taking his side." Dixie turned back and winked. "See you tonight, *Mrs. MacIntire.*"

FLYNN OPENED the side door to let Kean in. "Here," he said, holding up a gray suit. "It's all I've got. But you're two inches taller than me, so it's not going to work." He gave Flynn a disgruntled look. "Can't believe you didn't consider this till an hour before your own wedding reception."

Flynn took the coat from the hanger, parked his cane by the desk and shrugged into the jacket. The sleeves crawled two inches above his wrist. Kean shook his head. "BJ's going to kill you. A long slow painful death. She's a doctor. She can do it."

"We're just doing the reception to keep her mother and Grandma Mac happy. BJ won't care what I wear."

Kean raked a hand through his curly hair and chuckled. "You got the army thing down real good, little brother, but you don't know squat about women. We're talking *wedding* here."

"Once and for all, it's not a real marriage. It's just for—"

"Convenience. I got it. But if there's one thing I learned about women after being married to Shirley for ten years it's that women take their weddings serious and the reason for the wedding doesn't matter. Did you get BJ flowers?"

Flynn rolled his eyes. "Flowers? If there's one thing we don't need more of in this house it's flowers." He pointed out the window. "There's a whole damn yard filled with 'em. Why should I get her more?"

"You are so dead, army boy." Kean stuffed his hands in his pocket and rocked back on his heels. "What did you wear for your elopement? Jeans? A shirt with Go Army scrawled across the front?"

"A suit that fits. It's at the cleaners and they're closed and Clyde Imhoff's gone night fishing, damn his lucky hide, so there's no hope of him opening the shop to get my suit out."

Kean arched his left eyebrow just the way he always did before he and Flynn did something they'd be sorry for later. "Maybe we should break in and get it."

"Isn't that a bit extreme?"

"You show up at the reception in jeans and BJ will give you a whole new meaning for the word *extreme*. Where is she now?"

"Getting her hair done and nails and other girl stuff."

"Still think this reception doesn't matter?"

Flynn cursed, yanked off the suit jacket, grabbed the cane and headed out the door as his brother said, "We have to hurry. If you're late that won't do, either. BJ's first almost husband left her standing at the altar in front of the whole town. It wouldn't be nice to do that to her again."

"We're already married."

"But this reception makes it official and everyone will be there again."

He and BJ might not like each other all that much, but she didn't deserve another humiliation.

They drove a few blocks to Clyde's and pulled into the back alley. Flynn tried the rear door. He pushed his shoulder against it and shoved. Nothing. "It couldn't be that easy, would it! Now what?"

"Now we break in." Kean pointed to the roof. "Window's open in the attic. Give me a leg up."

"You can't climb with your hand. You'll just tear it open again and then BJ will really have my butt." Flynn held his cane like a baseball bat. "I'll smash the window and—"

A sheriff's cruiser pulled into the alleyway and Jack Dawson slid from behind the wheel. "What's up, guys?"

Flynn pointed his cane at the window. "I'm breaking into the dry cleaners to get my suit for the reception. If that doesn't work for you, lock me up. Least then I'll have an excuse for not being there."

Jack raised his hands in surrender. "Like hell. If I locked you up tonight and you missed this wedding reception, my ass would be grass and Maggie would be the lawn mower. No way, MacIntire."

Jack reached into his pocket and pulled out a key ring. "You're not the only man in this town to forget his suit at the cleaners. For the sake of marital bliss, Clyde gave me an extra key. Just leave the money on the counter."

Jack shoved the key in the lock as BJ rounded the corner, her hair and makeup perfect, her dress something right out of an expensive magazine—her face pinched and worried. Hell, he did that to her. He'd screwed this reception thing up big-time.

He said, "I apologize. I'm getting the suit right now.

I won't be late, I swear. How the hell did you know I was here? Marital radar?"

"Mrs. Homestead saw you out her back window and called to tell me my new husband was trying to break into the dry-cleaning store and was probably going to wind up in the pokey instead of at his wedding reception." BJ nodded to an apartment across the alley. "She figured you forgot your suit like half the other men in this town. But we've got bigger problems than your suit, MacIntire."

"Yeah, flowers? I didn't get you any of those, either."

"Drew's run away." BJ held out a paper. "He's been gone hours. The flag was up, and I went searching for the boys and I found Petey crying. Drew said he was running away because no one loved them and when he found a good home he'd come back for Petey."

"Does Katie have any idea what's going on?"

"Aunt Katie is nowhere to be found. I have no idea what's going on. The boys were supposed to be staying with a sitter, but she never showed up."

BJ suddenly slammed her small fist against the side of the building, making all three men jump in surprise at the calm, cool, controlled town doctor acting completely out of character and tearing the hell out of her delicate, perfectly manicured hand. *"Dammit to hell!* I should have done something about this sooner."

Kean took a handkerchief from his back pocket, turned the clean side out and wrapped it around her skinned knuckles. "We'll find him, Doc. Don't you worry now."

BJ shook her head. "He's seven years old and he's completely alone."

"We have a whole reception of people assembled to help us find Drew." Jack said. "I'll get the word out to the surrounding sheriff's offices and highway patrol and meet you at the country club in twenty minutes."

BJ followed Kean to his truck and slid across the dirt and mud left from MacIntire and Sons Construction jobs. Flynn knew zilch about dresses, but this one was ruined, he felt sure. It didn't bother BJ at all. In fact, the fashion diva of Whistlers Bend didn't even seem to notice.

Kean stopped in front of BJ's house and said, "I'll get supplies from my place and meet you at the reception."

Flynn followed BJ as she ran up the garden path, her high heels tapping across the brick. How could she run in heels? Normally, she couldn't run, period. She opened the door and said, "Give me five minutes and I'll—"

Then she stopped dead, staring at Drew's jacket, which hung on the coatrack by the door, probably left from the morning. "When I find him I'm going to wring his neck for worrying me like this. Petey said he rode his bike, so heaven knows where he went off to."

"Where's Petey now?"

"With Flo," BJ said in a lower voice. "I should have known this would happen, Flynn. I should have stepped in, done something sooner. Katie might be their aunt, but she's not up to raising two boys. I kept hoping she'd get better, but…but she's so young. Petey has special needs and Drew can be hell on wheels. It's too much."

BJ blamed herself for this. If something happened,

she'd never forgive herself. *God, he didn't want that for her, for anyone.*

He stood in front of her and looked her in the eyes. "Drew is definitely a handful and that's exactly why he's okay. He's tenacious and resourceful and—"

"He's you?"

"More or less."

"Something happened to set him off, Flynn. Petey won't say what, but it had to be big or Drew would never have left him. At least Drew had the good sense not to take Petey away from medical care."

"You've got five minutes, Doc. Dress warm. We should go."

She went to her room and Flynn to his. He pulled on his boots and grabbed his army field jacket, and stepped into the hall as BJ was coming out of her room, carrying what had to be a cashmere coat, matching gloves and hat that coordinated with her dark brown slacks and boots. Her hair, still braided on top of her head, and her pearl earrings, made her look as if she were headed for a night in New York.

"Not exactly an outfit for tracking in the woods, Doc."

"It's all I have. I don't track. Remember how the woods hate me? Bugs bite me, birds squawk at me, everything green and brown alike, I have no idea where I am. When the sign says No Trespassing it means me."

"I remember." He kissed her on the forehead, went back into his room and returned with his other field jacket. He held it out to her. "Not fashionable, but if it rains you won't get wet."

She swept her eyes from it to him. "You're enjoying this, aren't you? Me wearing olive drab."

He smiled. "Maybe a little."

She took the coat. "All right, but I'm buying you a blue shirt."

"As long as it's not navy."

She tossed her coat into his room, when it landed on his duffel bag, and they headed for the stairs. "We'll take my SUV." And fifteen minutes and a hair-raising drive later they walked into the country-club dining room. It was complete with white tablecloths, china, huge wedding cake, soft music, flowers, ice sculptures, sandwiches about the size of an ant's ear, drinks—and Margaret Fairmont totally furious.

She stormed over to them. "Barbara Jean, what is that thing you're wearing? How could you embarrass me like—"

"Not now, Mother. Drew Prescot's run away and we have to find him."

"That little ruffian who picks my apples every fall, rides through my sprinkler on his bike and puts tire tracks in my yard?"

Jack hustled into the room. The music stopped and everyone froze, staring at him, realizing something was up other than a wedding reception. "We have a missing boy," Jack called out. "Drew Prescot. And we need everyone to help look for him."

"I saw Drew riding his bike to beat the band about two hours ago," Harry Moran yelled. "When I was coming in from Sky Notch after visiting Maggie."

Flynn pulled duct tape from his jacket and fixed a

map to the wall as Jack continued. "Then we'll concentrate the search from Sky Notch and branch out."

Flynn motioned for everyone to gather close. "We'll work in a grid." He pointed his cane at the map. "Volunteer for the area you know best. Those of you who do mountain search-and-rescue understand the drill. Cover that area. The rest work in groups of three. Bring food and water with you, dress warm and wear hats and navigation equipment—don't need anyone getting lost. If you don't have radios or walkie-talkies, get one from Kean or the sheriff and keep in touch with him and one another."

Flynn paused, glanced at Jack as he nodded. "And if you see anything or anyone suspicious call it in," Flynn said. "There've been truckers driving the high roads and they aren't cattle haulers. We don't have any idea what's up, so don't be the hero and confront them."

"Butch and I'll take the south-west area by our farms," Dan Pruitt said. "We've got an outbuilding where Drew could be hiding if he needed to hole up for the night."

Maggie walked to the door, "I'll get my hands to cover Sky Notch. We've got about two hours of light left. Then we'll be down to flashlights."

"Better get a move on." Henry, Maggie's father, added. "Mighty small boy to be hunting with flashlights."

"And it's mighty big territory," Jack finished as he stared at the map.

BJ WRAPPED a bandage around Maggie's ankle, then handed her a glass of water and aspirin. Maggie said,

"I don't believe I sprained my ankle a month before my wedding. How could I trip over a log?"

"Usually, that's my line." BJ hugged her. "There's a good chance you'll be okay by then, but if not, *the bride wearing crutches* will give you and Jack something to talk about on your anniversaries."

Maggie gazed at her puffy ankle. "We were married for seven years, divorced thirteen and now we're getting remarried. We've got plenty to talk about already."

BJ checked the bandage, making sure the wrap wasn't too tight. "Well, now you have more." She helped Maggie off the table, steadied her and handed her the crutches just as Jack strolled in. He pushed his sheriff's hat to the back of his head and eyed his bride-to-be. "That's my girl."

"This isn't funny, Jack."

"Nope, but it's okay by me." He strolled across the room and scooped Maggie into his arms, the crutches crashing to the floor, and kissed her hard. "Anything that keeps you in my arms is damn perfect."

BJ smiled. "I called Billings Memorial and they're expecting you. They have better X-ray equipment and I want to make sure everything's okay."

Jack winked and retraced his steps, his soon-to-be bride cradled in his arms.

A pang of envy settled in BJ's heart. Her marriage consisted of a handshake. 'Course, there was the waiting-room incident to consider, but that wasn't love, that was...*an incident.*

"Hey," Flynn said from the doorway. "Busy?"

"Two sprains, one of them Maggie, five lacerations

requiring stitches. That's what happens when you have people running around in the night with flashlights and they don't know where they're going." She quirked her eyebrows. "No Drew? I didn't even get a chance to search for him."

Flynn parked his cane at the doorway and tramped into the examining room. Boots, field jacket, needing a shave, an army man through and through, and so darn handsome she clasped her hands to keep from touching him. He sat down on the stool by the treatment table. "Jack called off the search till tomorrow. Everyone's exhausted and they're starting to get careless. Some wedding reception."

"When we find Drew, it will be."

"You're dead tired, Doc. Pretty, but tired."

Her heart skipped a beat. "Pretty?"

"We're both too tired and worried about Drew to argue, so you'll have to settle for pretty and know I mean it."

She nodded to the kitchen. "You sure have a way with words, soldier. How about I buy you a beer?"

He followed her and turned for the fridge. "You sit," she said. "I'll make a sandwich. Your leg's got to be bothering you."

He held it out, moved it back and forth. "Not as bad as it could be. Maybe it's getting better in spite of me."

"It sure isn't getting better because of you."

He grabbed a map from his jacket, hung the cane on the edge of the table, then slipped the jacket off and put it on the counter. "Just what I need—a smart-ass at 0200 hours."

"To the rest of us that's 2:00 a.m." She spread her

arms wide. "Why can't army people just say 2:00 a.m.? What's the deal?"

He glanced up from the map. "Why can't you just say 0200 hours? What's the deal?"

She handed him a Coors. "If we were stranded on a desert island three feet wide we'd find something to argue over."

"Or…something." His words hung between them almost like a challenge.

"We can't go there, Flynn. It would never work. It didn't work twenty years ago, and not all that much has changed between us." She grabbed sandwich fare from the fridge because doing something was a lot easier than dealing with what could be but would never work.

He sat on a bar stool by the window and studied the map instead of her, probably for the same reason, taking a long drink of beer. "Here's your house." Flynn tapped the map. "Here's where Henry said Drew was riding his bike. No one's seen him since."

She stopped slicing a tomato and faced Flynn, a chill inching up her spine. "Do you think the truckers…?"

Flynn shook his head. "They're not after kids. They're hauling something, but who knows what. And they're meeting up at different places. The chances of Drew and these guys connecting are slim."

He studied the map again and pointed to Sky Notch. "Maggie and her hands covered the ranch. The teenagers searched the back areas up to Cabin Springs. Henry organized the seniors into driving the other roads and investigating the parks. Search-and-rescue did the mountains, though Drew couldn't have gotten very far in that direction before night fell."

Flynn ran his finger over the map. "This road forks by Sky Notch. The paved section heads west. The dirt road goes east to the old depot."

She piled ham and cheese on the bread. "Jack and his deputy looked there first. It's runaway central. Drew wouldn't have been the first kid here to get mad at his parents and hide out at the mine."

Flynn took another drink. "In junior high I got grounded for fighting the Trenton twins and ran off because I was pissed. Then I got hungry and came home and got grounded double."

"The Trenton twins." She shuddered as she sliced the sandwich into halves. "Those boys were pure evil. Always picking on somebody, mostly me. When I was twelve they pushed me off my bike and I got cut on some glass." She glanced at her forearm. "I still have the scar and…

She gazed at Flynn. Their eyes met and quiet filled the kitchen. "Funniest thing, after that day, neither of those rotten jerks ever bothered me again. Why do you figure that is, Flynn MacIntire?"

He shrugged and turned his attention back to the map. "Beats the hell out of me, Doc."

"And you think *I'm* a bad liar."

"I *know* you are. I'll grab a quick shower before I eat." He got his cane and headed down the hallway and BJ set the sandwich beside the map.

She considered the route Flynn had outlined. "Where the heck are you, Drew Prescot?"

She stared out the window at the crescent moon low in the sky, at the flag from the hideout hanging on the pole and— She snapped fully awake and pulled her attention from the flag to the map. "Oh, my, God. The hideout. Flynn's hideout."

The idea was a long shot and it was nearly 2:00 a.m. Flynn had put in a tough enough day without running after a hunch. She scribbled a *be back soon* note, which he would probably take for a medical emergency of some sort. Then she grabbed his field jacket from the counter and ran out the door.

Chapter Eight

BJ hit the accelerator and took a hard right. The SUV skidded from the paved road onto the dirt one, up to Silver Gulch. The car bounced over potholes and ruts and rocks till the old weathered train depot came into sight. The boarded-up mine lay to the left, an outcropping of trees and brush to the right. Flynn had said his hideout was close to the mine entrance, behind brush. And she'd look for that pine tree with two trunks.

She stopped the car, but kept the headlights on, shining at the spot where the cave might be. A flashlight would be good. Too bad that idea hadn't popped into her brain back at the house. Then again, BJ Fairmont did not venture out into the wilds of Montana ever, much less at 2:00 a.m.—or 0200 hours, as some thickheaded, though incredibly handsome, army man termed it.

Army man! His jacket. With so many pockets surely there'd be a flashlight. Duct tape, knife with enough tools to build a skyscraper, matches, nonscented candle—what a waste of a good candle—granola bars, flashlight. Ta-da!

She skimmed the light over the terrain, searching for disturbed grass or something. That was what they did on those *CSI* shows. If something sprang out or slithered or growled she'd die of fright.

She pushed aside bushes, and spotted an old pine with two trunks. Didn't bears live in caves? Bats? *Oh, God, bats.* Crouching, she held her breath—she had no idea why—aimed the light. She focused on an opening and looked inside to— "Drew!"

"Go away."

"Thank goodness you're okay." She felt light-headed with relief and held on to the cave wall for support, till something slithered across her hand.

She stifled a scream as Drew said, "Don't come here. I don't want you. I don't want anybody. Leave me alone."

He stood about ten feet into the shallow cave, his eyes huge, his face tear-stained, and he was shaking. As much as she wanted to run to him and wrap her arms around him, that had to wait. She needed answers; they had to get this straightened out. Something was terribly wrong, or Drew would never have left Petey. "Why did you run away?"

"I'm going to Billings to find a new home for Petey and me. They have shelters in cities and we could stay there. I saw some trucks up here and thought I could ask for a ride."

BJ's blood ran cold. "That's very dangerous. You know better than to take a ride with a stranger."

"You don't care about me! Nobody does."

"Of course I do. Most of the town's been looking for you. Where's Aunt Katie?"

"I hate, I hate her! She's sending me and Petey to foster people," he blurted. "I know what foster people are—seen it on TV. Petey and I might not even be together." His voice cracked. "They'll split us up."

"Drew, are you sure that's what Katie said?"

"Heard her talking to Eddie, that boyfriend. They went away for the day, but the babysitter never came. Eddie doesn't want kids. He hates rug rats. He calls us rats."

A tear slid down Drew's cheek. He sniffed and swiped it away with the back of his hand, leaving a dirty smear. "Aunt Katie doesn't want me or Petey and you don't, either," he sobbed.

Her heart cracked. "Of course I do."

His sad eyes met hers through the darkness. "You and Flynn want to adopt a baby. I heard you talking. *Why a baby?* Why can't you want to adopt me and Petey? *Why can't you love us?*"

Oh, God! The world stopped. She hadn't seen this coming, though she should have. What she said next mattered. *It mattered a whole lot to this little seven-year-old boy.* If she didn't say the right thing he'd be lost; he simply couldn't take any more rejection and being shuffled around, or acting brave for Petey. Drew was just a scared little boy. But she was a responsible adult, and it was Barbara Jean Fairmont's time to be brave and do the right thing…as her father would have. As she would do.

"I do love you," she said in a matter-of-fact voice, her mind made up. "I want you and Petey to live with me. I want to adopt you." It sounded good, very good.

"You're just saying that so I'll come back to town and—"

"Drew, have I ever, *ever,* lied to you? Haven't I always leveled with you, no matter what? You and Petey and me. We'll be a family, I swear."

"What about Flynn? You're married to him. What do we do with him? What if he doesn't want me?"

"Flynn will be a part of our lives, too. But he's going back to the army and won't be around as much. We'll bake him cookies, send him letters and pictures and silly cards, and sing to him on the phone and do e-mails on the computer. He can see us when he returns."

Drew paused for a moment and gave her a hard look, part of him wanting to believe, part of him afraid to. Disappointment did that, made you think nothing would go right again. Petey and Drew deserved better.

"You cross your heart? You really, really cross your heart?"

BJ put the light to her chest and made a cross. She extended her little finger. "And pinkie-swear."

"If you break a pinkie-swear your teeth fall out."

"I'm not breaking the promise. I'll talk to Aunt Katie tomorrow. I mean it, Drew." BJ held out her hand. "Petey's waiting for us. Let's go home."

"Home?" he said with a hint of hope, nearly breaking her heart more. His little finger wrapped around hers, feeling good and the right thing to do. Perfect. She hugged him, bringing his shivering body tight to hers. "Everything will be okay, Drew. We're all going to be fine."

She took off Flynn's jacket and wrapped it around

him, the thing dragging to the ground. "There. Now you're in the army. "

Drew stretched out his arms, sleeves hanging over his fingertips. He gazed down. "Neat." He smiled slowly, his eyes shining. "You won't go away?"

"If I have to go to medical conventions or into Billings for doctor things, Flo will take care of you till I get back. I'll call every night when I'm away."

"And bring back presents? Because that's what families do, right?"

"Yes, that's exactly what families do."

"Do you have anything to eat? I'm really hungry," he beamed and said.

She reached into the big pocket on the left side, pulled out a granola bar. "I think this is some kind of ration. If the army's attention to cuisine is anything like their attention to fashion I wouldn't expect too much."

His little face scrunched up. "What did you just say?"

She ruffled his hair and chuckled. "Nothing important." She ripped off the wrapper and handed it to him.

"Cool. Army grub. Army guys can do anything. They're tough. Flynn's tough. I bet Flynn can do anything."

BJ smiled. "Yeah, I think Colonel Flynn MacIntire can do just about anything. He's saved a lot of people in battle. Put himself at risk to do it. He's truly a hero."

"Bet he killed a lot of bad guys."

"That wouldn't be his first option, I'm sure." Killing would never be Flynn's first option.

Drew bit into the bar. "Why are you wearing his jacket?"

"That's what I want to know," said a voice from the entrance.

Drew ran to Flynn and threw his arms around his waist. "Doc BJ's going to adopt me and Petey and we're staying together and we're going to send you cookies and e-mails when you're in the army. Isn't that great?"

Still holding on to Flynn's middle, Drew rolled his eyes at him. "I'm eating one of your granola bars. Can I be in the army just like you when I grow up?"

This was not exactly how she'd intended to break the adoption news to Flynn. Even in the dim light she could see his eyes widen to the size of saucers. She imagined it took a lot to get that kind of response from an army colonel.

"Sure, Drew," Flynn said as he rubbed Drew's head, then brought the boy's little body close to his. "A soldier's a great thing to be."

He hooked his cane into his jeans pocket, shrugged out of his field jacket and handed it to BJ. She considered refusing but knew Flynn wouldn't wear a jacket if she didn't have one. That left him in a T-shirt with ARMY on it, which molded perfectly to his fine body.

Dear Lord, did he have to be so well built? At 0300 hours a resistance to Flynn didn't exist. Even a creepy cave with things crawling and slithering couldn't diminish her attraction to him.

She took the jacket, her fingers touching his, her insides blazing, her brain wondering why she kept feeling this way and wondering what she intended to do about it. "Thanks."

Drew snagged his bike, which sat propped against

the side of the little cave. "I'm really tired. Is Petey okay?"

"He's with Flo and he's fine." BJ helped Drew get the bike outside. She held Flynn's cane and he pushed the bike through the brush to her car and heaved it in the back. Drew jumped in, buckled up and finished off the granola bar. BJ made for the driver's side and came front to front with Flynn. *And he had such a nice front!*

He grasped her hand and stepped a few feet away. His expression suggested she needed therapy. "Adopt?"

"Hey, you're going to get cookies and e-mails. Don't complain."

"BJ?"

She exhaled. "Katie's putting Drew and Petey into foster care."

Flynn swore as she continued. "Those kids have been shoved from one home to the other in the past three years, Flynn. Their mother wasn't any prize and Katie isn't any better. I don't have a lot of options here, but this adoption idea is a good thing. It feels right to me. I wanted a child. Now I'll have two."

"Katie's nothing but a no-good, spoiled—"

"Drew and Petey are a lot of responsibility. Petey's condition alone makes the situation daunting to a young person, to any person. I'm a doctor. I can handle it better than most." She nodded at his car. "How did you find me?"

"Probably the same way you found Drew. Looked at the map and then at the flag, and *bingo,* everything fell into place. And I followed the skid marks. You need to slow down. Why didn't you get me?"

"You'd been out all day and I wasn't sure my hunch was right. And I don't drive fast—I drive with a purpose."

"BJ Fairmont, explorer and frustrated race-car driver. How are you going to manage a medical practice and raising two boys?"

"I'm going to manage my practice the same way other women handle their careers and family. One day at a time. It'll work. We better go." She turned for her car and he caught her arm.

"Do you have any idea what you've done? This is serious."

She pushed some wayward strands of hair back from her face. "You think I don't know that? Me taking them is their only hope, Flynn. They're out of options. It's foster care for them. Juvenile diabetes is incredibly expensive to deal with and is being picked up by insurance less and less. Taking Petey is more than expensive—it's the constant supervision and the fact that it's not going away. This is a lifetime condition. What do I do? Just sit around and hope Petey and Drew wind up together in a good home? I'm not doing that. I can't. If I'd hesitated for a moment to adopt Drew and Petey I would have broken Drew's heart. That little boy has had his heart broken enough."

Flynn's eyes darkened with realization. "You evened the odds."

"I'm really, really going to try. But you don't have to be a part of this. You didn't sign up to adopt two kids and a boatload of responsibility. We can get a quiet divorce. I'll talk to my attorney in the morning. You can still be part of the boys' lives, and I'll still work on your leg, of course, *if* and *when* you want." She nodded at the car. "But a baby's out of the picture. My plate's pretty full."

"You'll need help—a nanny and a cook and a gardener."

"I'll think about it."

His eyes hardened. "You've never been a mom. You're forty. You can't do this alone."

"Do you realize how many grandparents are raising their grandchildren these days because they have to? And I'm a lot younger than they are."

"But they were parents once. You're…a doctor."

"That counts for something. I can bandage a hurt knee."

"You can't wise-ass your way out of this."

"Humor might help. I know what if feels like to be kicked to the curb by someone you trusted, someone you loved—or at least, thought you did. Then your whole world blows up and you have no idea what to do."

"Randall Cramer?"

"And I was an adult when that happened. Petey and Drew are kids. I want better for them. I'll figure out how to make us a family as I go. Lighten up, soldier." She punched his arm, more amazed than ever how solid it was. "This is one of those happily-ever-after moments. Flowers bloom, birds sing, the kids find their way home—"

"To your house."

"If that's what makes them happy. Maybe us together was one of those things meant to be. I wanted a child and two found me." She stood on tiptoe and kissed him on the cheek. His breath warmed her all over. How'd he do that? "Don't be so worried."

"Your house, your life, isn't set up for two hell-on-wheels boys. Take it from one raised in a house of three hell-on-wheels boys."

"I'll call in Grandma Mac. She seems to have done okay with Scully and Kean." She patted his cheek. "The jury's still out on you."

"Like hell. I heard what you said to Drew back there." He hitched his chin at the cave.

She thought of saying, *Don't believe everything you hear,* but the words just wouldn't come out. "Then I guess the jury is in. See you back at the house."

She slid into the driver's side of the SUV, Flynn's eyes never leaving her. A slow heat flickered in their depths. She understood, knew what that meant. She also knew that anything of real substance between her and Flynn was out of the question. Not only did they argue, but they lived totally different lifestyles, and now their plans were as different as dawn and dusk.

She put the SUV in gear and slowly headed down the road, Flynn's car behind her. She called Jack and Flo on her cell, telling them about having found Drew but nothing about the adoption, as a pile of details had to get worked out. Jack would spread the word about Drew being safe and everyone in Whistlers Bend would rest a lot easier.

She parked in front of her house, undid Drew's seat belt and tried to pick him up. How could such a scrawny kid weigh so much?

"I'll do that," Flynn said, nudging her aside. He handed her his cane and scooped Drew into his arms. "I'll put him in my bed. I can use the couch."

She followed them up the walk, crickets and frogs performing a late-night—or more accurately, early-morning—serenade. "I can take the couch," she said. "Drew sleeps in my room." She opened the door for Flynn and he passed in by her, his body grazing hers, his scent floating around her, his presence filling the room as it always did.

"I'll let Drew sleep in my—"

"Are you two arguing again?" Drew said, rubbing his sleepy eyes and gazing at Flynn, then BJ. "Why are you always doing that? Are you going to leave? When people argue somebody leaves." He wiggled out of Flynn's arms and stood, his eyes brimming with tears. "BJ promised everything would be okay. So did you."

"We're all fine." BJ soothed. She looked at Flynn. "No more arguing. You can sleep in the guest bedroom. It's been redecorated, very…male."

She followed Drew upstairs, Flynn behind her, and the little parade entered the guest room. Drew's eyes widened. "This is cool. It's like a guy's place. Wait till Petey sees it. Where'd all those flower things go?"

BJ frowned. "The attic."

"Neat."

Flynn sent her a *gotcha* wink. Drew went in, lay down on the bed and closed his eyes. Flynn and BJ watched him for a minute, but the little boy didn't move. "Is he asleep?" BJ whispered.

She tiptoed in, slipped off the jacket, then his dirty

gym shoes and equally dirty socks. Flynn covered him with the other side of the bedspread, then grabbed his duffel and BJ's coat, which she'd tossed there. He followed her into her room.

Using two fingers, she handed the field jacket to Flynn, then shrugged hers off and handed that over. "I'm getting a shower. Would you be so kind as to shake these out in the backyard? If something's crawling around in the pockets I don't want to even know about it."

"I'll finish that sandwich I put in the fridge."

She took two steps toward the bath connected to her room, then turned back to Flynn. "Maybe we should get bunk beds?"

"I don't think so." He sent her a wicked wink and she swallowed, her eyes huge, her body suddenly on fire. What to do? Jump into bed with Flynn right now, or chicken out and run for the protection of the shower? Making mental chicken sounds, she went into the bathroom and closed the door.

THE BATHROOM DOOR closed behind BJ and Flynn wondered if she had any idea what she'd done. Not just turning down his advances—she knew exactly what that was about and had probably made the right decision, though every part of his anatomy disagreed. But about the adoption.

He remembered life at his house with three boys growing up. It was nothing like life at the pristine Fairmont house, with one little prissy girl. But if BJ *hadn't* taken the boys, what would have become of them? Nothing good, he'd bet on *that*.

He trotted downstairs and shook out the jackets as BJ had asked, then dropped them on the bed. He walked into BJ's closet to hang her coat up. He paused in the closet doorway.

Clothes. He'd never seen so many. Soft and feminine, hanging perfectly ordered: slacks, skirts, dresses; tans, blacks, yellows and blues. Shoes on racks, purses above on a shelf. Not pretentious or flashy clothes, but simple, classic, elegant. Like Barbara Jean Fairmont. Her scent settled around him and he inhaled, breathing her deep into his lungs.

He wanted her right now, all warm and giving under him and her wanting him. But they were too stuck in their ways—he a soldier, she a doc. Agreeing on nothing. Battles didn't belong in a relationship but a war, and they couldn't seem to get beyond that.

He spied blankets and a pillow on the top shelf, brought them down and walked back into the bedroom. Water ran in the bathroom as he placed his duffel on the bed, picked out a pair of cotton drawstring pants, stopped in the bathroom to change and wash up, then headed for the couch. He bypassed the kitchen, too tired to eat.

An open window let in cool mountain air, and he spread the bedding over the cushions and across the back in case it got cold. The soft leather welcomed him and he fell into a deep sleep, till he heard, "There you are."

He pried one eye open. BJ. Dream or reality? Either was a definite improvement of the usual war scenes.

He blinked. Reality! And the moonlight creeping through the window silhouetted her, making him more awake by the minute. "Why are you here? Is there another emergency?"

"Oh, Lord, I hope not. But there is a bug in my room. The field jackets were on my bed."

"I shook them out, and guess someone liked them as much as I do."

"I don't think so, because he slithered out and is scurrying about my room. I can't sleep in there. I'll trade you places, okay?"

She wore a dark robe. It was open in the front, exposing a matching nightgown with a scooped neck that hinted cleavage and tied under her breasts. Her hair hung long and loose, gleaming in the faint light. She looked like a renaissance queen. "We have a predicament. I have the couch."

"It's my couch."

"I'm way too tired to argue tonight. In fact, right now arguing's the very last thing I want to do with you." He grabbed her around the thighs, pulling her off balance and toward him.

Her arms flailed, her eyes widened. He wrapped his other arm around her as she toppled onto him. Her eyes stared into his, wide, green, mysterious. "We both win. Isn't this better than arguing?"

Her breaths came fast and shallow. Her cheeks were flushed. "I don't know."

"Yes, you do." The flimsy material of her nightgown glided across his bare chest, then he stroked her hair and kissed her. She tasted of mint toothpaste and a flavor uniquely Barbara Jean Fairmont. His tongue engaged hers in tag; lost; won, then played again. Her warm hands framed his face; her lips were full and moist under his. She pulled her head back. Panting she said, "Maybe we'll both lose. What about that? Our relationship is all sex."

He arched an eyebrow. "I'm not complaining."

She slid from his grasp and stood as he said, "I want to make love to you, BJ, and it's what you want, too. The way you respond to my touch. I can tell."

"But that's physical. What about the rest? What about in here?" She touched her head.

"We'll work on it. Maybe it will happen—maybe it won't. But right now we're doing pretty good."

She stood there for a moment as if deciding what to do. Then she slipped the robe from her shoulders, letting it float to the floor. His insides tightened; his heart soared. She'd done this for him and that made this moment perfect. She wanted to give him pleasure and he wanted to give her pleasure in return.

Anticipation flowed though him, making him desire her all the more. "I'm glad you agree."

With no robe to contain it, the scent of her drifted to him as she undid the ribbon under her breasts, freeing the gathered material there. She pushed the nightgown from one shoulder, then the other, and it floated down her frame, exposing firm breasts, narrow waist, the gentle indent of her navel and the mysterious patch of silk at the juncture of her legs. The fabric pooled at her ankles and she stepped over it, bringing herself into a shaft of golden light.

His insides burned; his heart hammered against his ribs. She wore a glint in her eyes, a siren's smile and nothing else. "You never cease to amaze me, or turn me on."

Prickles of alarm crawled up his spine. "What about Drew? What if…"

"I just checked on him. Completely zoned out. Running away is hard work."

"And not just for him. And there's that squeaky stair that's better than an alarm system. If he comes searching for us we'll hear."

She gave Flynn a sassy wink. "You're getting to know my house pretty well." Her voice turned smokey as she added, "I'd like to get to know you the same way."

She sat on the edge of the couch, the buttery leather accommodating her, and placed her delicate hand on his chest, the scrapes across her knuckles still red from punching out Clyde's store. He kissed the back of her hand. "You shouldn't have done that."

"This from the man who's undoubtedly been in more fights than I could possibly imagine."

"Yeah, but fighting's not you."

"You don't understand me as well as you think you do, Flynn MacIntire. If I want something I fight for it, too."

Her fingertips roamed across his shoulders, up his neck, across his face. She leaned forward, gliding her hardening nipples across his chest. She lingered, her eyes meeting his, then she kissed him deep this time, her tongue telegraphing exactly what she hungered for.

He caressed her silky back as she laid a line of kisses down his middle. Her tongue tantalized his navel and desire twisted his gut. His arousal thrust against her breasts.

"You're the one naked," he murmured. "And I'm the one being seduced."

"My turn." Then her mouth found his erection through the thin material of his pants and he nearly fell off the couch. "BJ!"

Her lips formed to him; her wet tongue tormented him. He gripped the sides of the couch, fighting for control, and when her clever hands snuck under his waistband he nearly lost it.

"Enough, woman," he rasped. In self-defense, and because he needed to have his hands on her, he tossed the blanket across the back of the couch to the floor, gripped her shoulder and flipped her over, breaking the fall with his free hand. He braced himself on his elbows and stared into her startled eyes.

"You're a vamp in a lab coat." Than he ravaged her mouth in a mind-numbing kiss that nearly reduced him to ashes.

Her breasts swelled against him, her body dampened with excitement and her hands went to his back, her fingers pressing into his flesh. He broke the kiss. Breathless, he stood and stripped off his pants, then looked down at her, stretched out before him. "There is something about this waiting room."

"And us being together in it. Must be the seductive aroma of alcohol and antiseptic."

He laughed. Her hair was mussed, her breathing quick and erratic, her eyes bright with passion. "Damn, you are beautiful."

"Damn, so are you." She crooked her finger in come-here fashion.

Every part of him was taut. He pulled himself over her, loving the feel of her skin on his.

"Oh, Flynn," she said in a whisper that touched his heart. "I want you so much."

She wrapped her legs around his middle and he entered her in one thrust, taking her gasps into his mouth. He pushed deeper, then again and again. The exquisite pleasure of having her drove him beyond his limit and he climaxed as she did, making the world around them suddenly perfect beyond his wildest imagination.

"Too fast," he murmured in her ear. "I want days of this, weeks of this, BJ, not just twenty minutes on the floor of your waiting room. I want more—I want longer."

"I happen to think you're built just right for me. Longer wouldn't be good. And right now I want a bed."

He scooped his hands under her, caressing her, and rolled BJ and himself over, her body relaxed against his now. "I get sass from the town doctor."

"You get a lot more than that, Colonel." She winked.

He smiled. "How can anyone feel so wonderful, be just right for me?"

"Remember that tomorrow, when all hell breaks loose around here."

"Your mother. It will be interesting."

"Drew and Petey aren't exactly the country-club set." BJ lifted her head and gazed down at him, the afterglow of their lovemaking glazing her eyes, her lips full and fleshy from his kisses, her eyes misty.

"I'll stay around till things calm down. Everyone in town will want to know what's going on. You have office hours in the afternoon, and you'll have to deal with Katie sometime."

"I'll manage. Flo will help and I can always call in reinforcements. Dixie and Maggie will come in a flash if I need them and—"

He kissed her. "Changing the subject is one way to stop an argument. Your mother goes into overload when you wear olive drab. Adopting two kids might do her in. Dixie and Maggie aren't pushovers, but dealing with your mother could require more. A united front goes a long way in winning the war."

"She'll have to deal, Flynn. This has to happen. Those kids need me, need us. I'll make an appointment with my attorney about the adoption and you can talk to him about getting a divorce."

He ran a hand over his head. "There's a lot going on right now. Let's give it a few days. I'll be around for a while."

She rolled off him and pointed to the couch. "You stay here tonight. I'll take it tomorrow night." She picked up a corner of the blanket. "And we shouldn't have a repeat performance of this if we're talking divorce. I doesn't seem right without a commitment and neither of us is into that."

She snagged her nightgown and slipped it on. He handed her the robe. "See you in the morning, Doc."

He watched her walk off. "Hey," he called. "What about the bug? Want me to come kill it for you?"

She stopped and made a face. "No way. You and me near a bed is dangerous territory. I'll deal. I got the feeling I'm going to be doing a lot of that very soon." She shuddered. "But I really do hate bugs."

Chapter Nine

The first rays of morning brightened the room as Flynn felt something plop on his back, then something land on his ass. "Why are you sleeping on the couch, Flynn?" Petey said above him. "You and BJ are married, and married people sleep in the same room."

He could use a good excuse right now. "Why aren't you in school?"

Two little boys' laughs filled the room. "It's summertime, Flynn. No school."

Bad excuse. He could try again. "I couldn't sleep so I came down here. I didn't want to wake BJ."

"Why are her slippers here?" Petey asked.

"The slippers are mine."

The boys laughed again. "You have slippers with flowers on them?"

Flynn opened his eyes wide and focused on the slippers, which was obviously not his. He needed coffee, lots of it, and a cigarette or two or five. He looked at Petey. "How'd you get here? Thought you were at Flo's."

"I'm not anymore because you adopted me. Remember?" He giggled. "Drew told me this morning. He ran over to get me, and Flo gave me my shot and made us breakfast."

A piece of paper suddenly appeared in front of Flynn's face, too close to read. "I found this list of exercises for you to do," Drew said. "They were on the fridge. It says For Flynn."

Drew bounced up and down on Flynn's back. "Petey and I will go with you so your leg will get better and you can play baseball with us. I love baseball. I want to be a catcher."

Flynn growled, and Petey said, "You must be hungry. Your tummy's making noises."

"The sun's barely up, guys. Go back to bed."

"It says on the paper the first exercise is to stretch your legs and arms and back," Drew said. "Then walk five blocks without the cane. You can do that. You can do anything—BJ said so. Soon you'll get back in the army, 'cause that's where you belong. You can be a soldier again. Soldiers are the best. We'll write you letters."

Flynn wanted sleep. He wanted quiet. *He wanted a damn cigarette.* Drew and Petey slid off his back and butt and sat down on the floor in front of him, list in hand. Drew asked, "Are you ready to get up, Flynn? We're going with you 'cause Petey's supposed to exercise, too, and I want to be in the army when I get big. We'll all exercise together."

Just what Flynn deserved—a big dose of guilt to start off the morning. If he didn't go the boys would be devastated, Petey wouldn't get his exercise and Flynn wouldn't have two kids smiling ear to ear. Okay, he'd walk around the block, satisfy the boys, then take off for the Cut Loose for a well-rounded breakfast with the *ine* twins—caffeine and nicotine.

He sat up and Drew's eyes twinkled. "You're all hairy, Flynn. When do Petey and me get to be hairy like that? Girls aren't hairy."

"Hairy?" He could do exercises, go with little sleep and tolerate kids on his back, but this little conversation had all the earmarks of one of those birds-and-bees talks. He was not getting into *that.*

"Hi," BJ said from the hall. Flynn stood. "Ah, just what we need, a doctor."

Her eyes narrowed. "Someone hurt?"

"The boys here want to know when they're—"

"Going to get all hairy like Flynn." Drew grinned.

BJ folded her arms and peered at Flynn. "So tell them."

"They want the scoop about…*men.*"

She held out her hands. "I am not a man. That would be you."

Oh, hell. BJ did not look like a man. She looked soft and warm, in dark brown slacks and a cream-colored sweater, and he knew he was a man because he wanted to rip that damn thing off—except, they had company. Little company. "No, you're not a man, but I can't do this. I have no idea how to do this."

He took her hand, led her to the couch and sat her in front of the boys. He made for the hallway.

"Where are you going?" she called after him.

"To get my gym shoes." *Anything to escape.*

"Then we're going for a walk for Flynn's leg," Drew offered.

"He agreed?" BJ said, then laughed after him. "Well, having the boys here, asking all sorts of questions, is one way to get you to exercise. Too bad I didn't think of it earlier."

He swung his head around and caught her giving him a little salute.

"You're enjoying this, aren't you?"

"As much as you enjoyed me wearing that field jacket." Her eyes twinkled; her face was radiant. The kids sitting at her feet—this was the perfect setting for her. And—surprise, surprise—he liked being here to see it.

Flynn took the stairs to BJ's bedroom for his shoes. The yellow sheets were still rumpled, and the pillow was still indented where she'd slept. He touched the covers. Warm…like BJ. *He wanted her again*. Right now. But they'd decided this sexual attraction led nowhere, so what was the point?

He touched her pillow and his groin throbbed. *Damn*. He had to get better and get out of here, or he'd die of sexual frustration in no time.

He pulled his shoes from his duffel, put on a pair of sweats, left his cane by the door and made his way back downstairs. "We'll get our jackets and be back in a jiffy, Flynn," Drew said.

Flynn stared at BJ. "Okay, what did you tell them?"

"Why, Colonel MacIntire, are you needing pointers on being a *man?*"

He grabbed her and kissed her, her taste, her texture,

her aroma, overwhelming him. He broke the kiss and she stared at him, dreamy eyed and flushed. "I'll take that as a no." She licked her lips and he kissed her again.

"Flynn." She seemed startled, excited, hungry, fighting with herself to let him go. "I told the boys that when they started sounding like a man, they'd start looking like a man."

"That's it?"

"They don't want an anatomy lesson. Just a simple answer."

"Right. Simple answer. I'll remember that."

"We're ready," Drew yelled as he ran down the hall.

"Wait," BJ said, holding up her hands and bringing the boys to a tumbling-on-the-floor halt. Little boys spent as much time on all fours as they did upright. "First," she said, "no running in the house. That's for outside. And the same with yelling. Sick people come here and they don't need noise. We have to all help them feel better."

The boys nodded, their expression as if BJ had just asked them to donate a kidney. As they all walked to the side door Flynn said to her, "Call Scully and Kean."

"Because you're going to be late?"

"Because your house is shrinking. Ask for the MacIntire discount, since you are legally a MacIntire."

"I need an addition?"

"Doc, you need an office." He winked and went out the side door.

An hour later he came back in the side door. Or, more accurately, he *hobbled* back in, then *hobbled* up the steps, heading for the shower. He hurt in places he didn't know he had, and he'd kept up a good front the whole damn time because the boys were with him.

No more heading off to the Cut Loose instead of exercising, no more sneaking cigarettes in the kitchen by the open window. He had witnesses, two, running around him in circles, telling him funny stories and giggling, asking him about the army. Damn, how could he grumble or cut his exercises short or smoke with hero worship oozing from every one of their little pores?

The boys were spreading the word about the adoption and he felt sure that his name was part of the news. As much as he'd never planned on being their dad, he was. And it was just fine.

He turned the shower to hot, stripped and stepped in, the heat soothing his muscles, but not as much as he'd hoped. He still hurt, and he mumbled swearwords as he flexed his leg and stayed in the shower till the water ran cold. He snagged one of his big brown totally guy towels and wrapped it around his middle, his leg feeling more like a hunk of wood than flesh. He went into the hall and faced BJ.

She peered at him the way doctors do, making him feel as though he had leprosy. "You look awful."

"You have the worst bedside manner. You should work on that. Subtlety is good. Try it sometime."

"This from a man who drives a tank? Did you stretch before you walked?"

He growled, his leg burning. "It was a walk, BJ. You don't stretch for a walk and I don't want a lecture."

"You should follow orders." Her hair was piled on

top of her head, showing her long neck. She looked terrific and he knew exactly what he needed.

She knelt in front of him and ran her hand up his injured leg. "Your muscles are in knots. They're stiff and
strained."

Her hands massaged his leg. The more she kneaded
his flesh, the better he felt, until suddenly more than his
leg was stiff and strained. He gazed down at her golden
hair, her capable hands making mincemeat out of his
self-control.

"BJ."

"Just a minute, I'm working out the knots and—"

He took her arms and lifted her in his. Then he kissed
her as she melted against him, her arms around his
neck, her breasts firm against his chest, her mouth sweet
and wet to his. He carried her to the bathroom and set
her on the counter, kicking the door shut with his bad
leg.

"What are we doing?"

"Having sex and keeping the kids out in case they re-
appear. They stopped at Ms. Millie's for juice." He
planted the words against her lips.

"Thought we weren't going to do this."

"We lied." He yanked off his towel, then bunched her
skirt to her thighs and he pushed aside the slip of silk
between her legs, leaving her open and inviting. She
gasped, her head dropping back as she breathed his
name and closed her eyes, pleasure softening her face.
His pulse drummed. "You are so tight, so silky."

She spread her legs wider, fueling his own need for
her, and he pumped into her, strong steady strokes as

she gave her body to him. A roaring sound filled his ears, and he pushed into her once more and held her tight as they climaxed, her body shuddering against him.

"Oh, Flynn," she said at his neck, nuzzling him. "How are we going to stop this?"

He kissed her hair. "Maybe we shouldn't try."

"Then what? You go back to the army, come here a few times a year and we have great sex?"

"Okay. I can do that." She pursed her lips and he sighed. "You're right. You deserve better and so do I, but we are married—"

"Sort of. Argue by day and have sex at night isn't my idea of a happy family life."

He stepped away as little footsteps thundered on the stairs. His eyes widened and BJ slid off the counter. "Oh, no."

She pulled back the shower curtain, pushed him in, grabbed his towel and tossed it in after him, then slid the curtain home.

"BJ," said Drew from the hallway. "Your mom's here."

BJ CURSED AND CLOSED her eyes. "Now what?"

Flynn whispered from behind the curtain, "I'll be down in a minute. We should face her together. We're allies."

"Battle of the kitchen. But this isn't your fight. I'll handle my mother."

"I'll be there as soon as I grab some clothes."

BJ opened the door, thinking how much she'd rather

he'd grab her, instead. Except, that couldn't happen again. This nonsense had to end.

It was fantastic being with Flynn. Being forty and having sex went together real well, especially with Flynn as the other half! She glanced in the mirror and ditched her I-love-sex expression to put on her I-am-Mommy expression, then stepped into the hallway. She closed the door behind her.

"Who were you talking to in there?" Petey asked, pointing to the bathroom.

"Singing, just singing…as I cleaned." Pretty good explanation and not exactly a lie. She'd picked up a towel—that was cleaning—and having sex with Flynn was musical, sort of like the finale of the 1812 Overture—cannon, fireworks, explosions. Big explosions. Forget explosions. She had a catastrophe to deal with.

"My mother's downstairs?"

"She was coming up the walk so we're here to get you," Drew said. He made a face as if he'd eaten a lemon. "She's kind of scary looking, BJ."

"Her bark's worse than her bite."

"She barks and bites!" the boys said together, totally freaked out.

BJ held up her hands. "No, that's an expression. My mother would never do either of those things."

"We told everyone in town about the adoption. Ms. Millie said you had her deepest sympathy. Is that another one of those expressions?"

BJ squelched the urge to strangle Ms. Millie and smiled, instead. "That's her way of saying she's happy we'll be together."

BJ took the boys' hands in hers and led them toward the stairs. They were in this together and Margaret needed to know that.

"Hello, Mother," BJ said as she entered the kitchen.

Margaret frowned. "So, you're really going to adopt?"

"Good morning, Margaret," Flynn greeted her.

Margaret looked from BJ to him. "And neither of you found the time to call me about this little incident. First the marriage and now—"

"I was working on the legalities this morning," BJ said. "It's been a little hectic around here, but now—"

"So, these are soon to be my *grandchildren?*" Margaret said, walking around the boys, observing their way-less-than-perfect appearance—dirty clothes, smudged faces, unkempt hair, grungy gym shoes. Things Margaret would never have tolerated in BJ, or her mother would have tolerated in her. Old money had old sophistication and a certain class.

"Yes, they are," Flynn said from the doorway.

"Well," Margaret stated as BJ held her breath, hoping her mother would be nice, even though these were definitely not the grandchildren she'd envisioned. "I believe these boys are two of the finest young men I've ever seen in all my life."

BJ blinked. "What?"

Margaret huffed. "*What* is not acceptable grammar, Barbara Jean. It's *excuse me* if you've misunderstood."

Misunderstood! Try flabbergasted.

Margaret put one hand on each of the boys' shoulders in a possessive gesture that brought tears to BJ's eyes. Margaret gazed from one to the other. "I am to be your grandmother now."

Petey's eyes widened. "You are?"

"Indeed. I've wanted grandchildren for years and years and now I have you and you have me. I think we can make this work. Don't you?"

Drew nodded and Petey followed. Margaret nodded back and sat on a bar stool—*she never sat on bar stools*—and lifted Petey into her lap. His dirty jeans slid across a four-hundred-dollar Armani skirt. Then she brought Drew close to her side. "There. That's better."

She reached into her purse, plucked out a camera and held it out to Flynn. "I bought it this morning. Made Zack Little open his hardware store for me early to get it. Told him I was a future grandmother and needed pictures of me together with my future grandsons. I'm going for lunch at the Woman's Club in Billings and want to pass around pictures. It's my turn." She smiled, her eyes suddenly dancing. "It's actually my turn." She hugged the boys closer. "I couldn't be happier."

Flynn looked as though he'd seen a ghost, and BJ felt weak and sat down on the other bar stool. Margaret said to the boys, "Stand and sit tall, chins up. You're soon to be Fairmonts."

The boys hiked their little shoulders back, a proud expression on their faces. Margaret Fairmont appeared… happy. *Incredible.*

Flynn snapped pictures till the boys were dizzy from the flash. "Now," Margaret said to Drew and Petey, "I'm taking you to meet your grandma Mac. She should be finishing up her tae kwon do class, and then we'll go shopping. Grandma Mac is having us all for dinner—stuffed cabbage, I believe. We'll get clothes first, then perhaps toys are in order."

BJ stood. "Mother, you shouldn't bribe the boys to behave."

Margaret tipped her chin. "Nonsense. Of course I should. *You* shouldn't, dear." She smiled sweetly and patted her cheek. "Grandmothers get to do anything. License to spoil, at least a little from time to time."

The boys yelped and jumped up and down until Flynn said, "Drew, Petey. No more. You are to go upstairs, make your beds, shower and put on the clean underwear, jeans and shirts that your aunt Katie sent over for you."

Drew and Petey froze and Drew asked, "Is she going to take us back?"

"No," BJ said. "But she'll visit here and you can visit her. We had a talk. Is this okay with you?"

The boys nodded.

"Good," BJ said, feeling that things were slowly falling together.

"And you two will behave and mind your manners when you are with your grandmothers," Flynn added.

BJ held her breath. This was a lot to dump on the kids at one time. The boys stood there for a moment, wide eyed. Truly one of those sons-meets-father moments, or boys-meets-colonel moments. Drew made a face. "What happens if we don't?"

Flynn's eyes darkened. BJ hoped Flynn remembered to keep the answer simple. "You are now a part of this house, this family," he said, "and it's your responsibility to take care of the people here and the home you live in."

"That's what army men do, right?" asked Drew.

Flynn nodded, and Drew and Petey ran, then walked, down the hall.

Margaret laughed. "Ah, the voice of a man. Nothing quite like it. Well done, Colonel."

Flynn held out his hand to Margaret. "And the way you welcomed the boys was…astounding. I'm overwhelmed."

She smiled and blushed. "Why, thank you." She turned her attention to BJ "And the adoption process will take place without a hitch?"

"Katie is relieved and grateful she can still be part of the boys' lives. The adoption is going to be fine. The adoption won't be final for a year, but everyone seems happy with the decision."

"If you require my help, dear, just ask."

BJ embraced her mother—something she hadn't done nearly enough lately, but she intended to change that, too. "Now," BJ said. "I should give you both a lesson in childhood diabetes."

Margaret looked stricken. "Oh, my. Which one?"

"Petey. We need to monitor his diet, insulin and exercise. You'll have to give him shots if you're away from me. I'll show you how to take care of him if there's a problem."

Margaret squared her shoulders. "I can do this. I was married to a doctor, helped him out on several occasions."

BJ bit back a laugh. She didn't remember seeing this

side of her mother. Then again, her father had been around to manage things. Twenty min-utes later BJ felt confident Margaret and Flynn had a working knowl-edge of at least the basics, provided they stayed in town and BJ was a phone call away. She'd do more later.

Drew and Petey bounded into the kitchen, grinning and clean, hair standing on end.

"We're ready." Drew held out a wallet to Margaret. "Petey and I got this for you since you're our grandma and all. We'll pick roses from BJ's garden for Grandma Mac."

Grandma? Margaret Fairmont as Grandma! Boggled the mind.

Margaret smoothed down their hair, then took the wallet. "Louis Vuitton. My, my."

BJ studied Drew. "Where did you get this?"

"I didn't steal it." He pouted defensively. "I wouldn't do that."

BJ put her arm around him. "I'm not accusing you, Drew. I just asked. That's all. This wallet is not sold in any stores in Whistlers Bend and it's very expensive."

"Actually," Margaret interrupted, "it's not. It's a knockoff."

Drew's eyes opened wide. "Knockoff? That's what happens in the movies when somebody shoots some-body. I didn't shoot nobody to get that wallet."

Flynn stooped beside Drew. "Knockoff means not the real thing."

Drew looked at Flynn as if he'd lost his mind. "It's real. It's right there. I can touch it."

Flynn bit back a smile and said to Drew, "It's real but

not authentic. Like, if some kid at school tried to sell you a baseball signed by Babe Ruth for a quarter. What would you think?"

"That he was a lying jerk and the name wasn't real." A light of understanding sparked his big brown eyes. "I found the wallet behind the depot when I was searching around for Flynn's hideout. Then I saw some trucks came and I got scared and ran back into the trees and found the hideout then."

Fear crawled up BJ's spine and Flynn took Drew's hand. "Did the men in the truck see you?"

"I took the wallet for Petey for a present and put it in my pocket. Then we decided it was too girlie 'cause it was blue, and we should give it to Grandma Fairmont 'cause she dresses real pretty."

BJ knelt down. She swallowed hard. Scaring the boys was not what she wanted to do. "Are you sure no one saw you? This is very important."

Drew shook his head. "I was just looking around. I didn't hurt anything and the wallet was just there, like somebody dropped it."

Flynn put his hand on Drew's shoulder. "You did good, pal. Real good." He held up the wallet and said to Margaret, "A knockoff? Looks pretty expensive. Maybe it *is* the real thing. One of the high-school kids could have dropped it out there."

Margaret's eyes narrowed a fraction and she pulled herself up tall and peered at Flynn. "Would I question you on the appearances of a *tank*."

Flynn held up his hand in surrender. "Right. I apologize."

"Besides," Margaret continued, "the sleeve with the registration is in here. If someone had purchased the wallet they would have taken this out, even if it was a knockoff. This piece as a real Louis Vuitton would sell for over four hundred dollars."

Flynn let out a low whistle; the boys' eyes rounded. "Wow."

"A fake like this one would go for maybe thirty-five from an unscrupulous street vendor. Not only do the designers like Louis Vuitton and Gucci and the rest lose revenue on products they've designed, but our country is robbed of the taxes, and the knockoffs are often made overseas in sweatshops that exploit children. Ugly business, knockoffs.

"Here," Margaret said. "I'll show you how to tell a fake. The sleeve for the registration card isn't a true camel color. It's too muddy. The embossed LV on the front is slightly smudged, not crisp. A stitch at the corner is askew, not perfect. And the blue shade is a tad off."

She tsked and threw her hands in the air. "Louis Vuitton would spit on such a wallet."

Petey's eyes shone bright. "Would he really? Does Louis live around here? Drew and me are the best spitters in town. We can have a spitting contest."

Margaret smiled. "Louis is in New York. I'll take you to visit him when you're a little older, but no spitting." She tilted her head. "On second thought we'll go before school starts. We'll visit Louis and you can pick me out one of his real wallets. Then we'll visit the Statue of Liberty. We'll stay at the Waldorf, liven the place up a bit. Tends to get a bit stuffy. Now, go outside and wait by my car. I'll be along in a moment."

Drew said in an awed breath, "They have a baseball team in New York. The Yankees. They're the best, Petey."

The boys ran out the door, talking about baseball and visiting Louis. BJ took her mother's shoulders. "Have you really considered this? Drew and Petey in New York? They're a little rambunctious for Whistlers Bend? The Waldorf! Oh, Mother, the Waldorf?"

Margaret laughed and headed for the door. "I know. The place may never be the same. In fact, I'm sure it won't. And the best part is neither will I. I've never been to a baseball game. I imagine I'll have to buy peanuts in a bag and throw shells on the ground. Who would have thought?"

BJ watched the door close, then said to Flynn. "What's gotten into her? Is she okay? She's not the same person she was yesterday. Maybe it's medical."

"It's grandchildren." Flynn chuckled. "Grandma Mac once said that if she knew how much fun grandchildren were she would have had them first." He put the wallet in his pocket.

She winked. "Either you're accessorizing and the army is in for a big shock, Colonel MacIntire, or you're taking the wallet to Jack."

He walked to her, a flicker of fire in his eyes as he slid his arm around her middle. He brought her body to his and kissed her. She kissed him back, then stepped away because she was a damn fool.

"We can't do this," she panted. "Not that it isn't

great." She closed her eyes for a moment. "Oh, it's really great, Flynn, but— "

"A sexual fling isn't you, and the fact that we are married isn't going to change things, is it?"

"What's your opinion of waiting awhile for the divorce? The boys have enough to deal with at the moment with their lives being uprooted. Maybe after you go back to the army and things settle down, then we can set the legal wheels in motion."

Flynn gave her that confident stance he did so well when he knew he was right. "Doc, you got two boys living with you now. Settling down isn't going to happen for about twenty years or so. We can work out the divorce whenever you think best. I'd like to set up a trust fund for Drew's and Petey's education. Not that you can't afford it—" he rushed on before she could jump in "—but because I want to continue to be part of their lives."

He winked. "And as for sex… If you change your mind, I'm here."

The door closed behind him. *Let him know?* She checked her watch. Only forty-five minutes since they'd had sex in the bathroom and she wanted it—*him*—again, now.

She had to get over this. She had to take their marriage for what it was—an opportunity to adopt children and give Flynn the kick in the butt to get better. Mission accomplished—time to move on.

The doorbell sounded. The front door? No one came to the front door. It was going to be one of *those* days. She opened the door and three young men stood on the little porch. "'Morning, ma'am. Is this the residence of Bear, uh, I mean Colonel Flynn MacIntire?" He nodded at the men to his side. "We're three of his unit leaders."

"Flynn MacIntire lives here. I'm his—" *What? Arguing partner, sex partner, pain-in-the-butt acquaintance?* She went with "—wife. He isn't in, but you're welcome to wait. He should be back soon, I think."

The soldier chuckled. "Bear's like that. Can never quite figure what he's up to. If it wouldn't be too much trouble we'd like to see him."

She led the way down the hall to the waiting room. "Have you had breakfast?"

"On the drive in from Billings, ma'am."

All three sat on the couch. She sat across from them in a chair, feeling the room shrink by half. No out-of-shape males here. The tallest handed her a box wrapped in wedding paper. "From some of the troops. Didn't want the colonel to forget us—we sure won't forget him. How's his leg, ma'am— if you don't mind me asking, that is?"

"Better."

The one solder nudged the other. "Told you Bear would be back."

"Why do you call Flynn 'Bear'?" BJ asked.

"Nickname, ma'am. Big Bear. Takes no sh—I mean grief from anyone and watches after his own." He touched his brass belt buckle. "When we were deployed the colonel gave each of his unit leaders one of these with *Above the rest* stamped on the back. Then we went out and got tanks tattooed on our right arms and got stinking drunk."

The middle soldier added, "The troops started calling him Bear when he tore through a burning building and yanked out two of his men, just like a mama bear."

The third soldier said, "I heard he got the name when he pulled that kid out of that river and looked like a drowned bear." They all laughed. Just then Flynn strode into the room.

The men stood. "Colonel."

Flynn's face broke into a wide grin. "What the hell are you guys doing here? Who's fighting the war?"

"How are you getting on? When are you coming back?"

"Soon." His face brightened and she'd never seen him so confident or in his element. He was a stranger in her house. With these fine men he was at home; they were family. They had a bond, just as she did with her patients. A bond that cut through the junk and went right to life and death.

"I'll get coffee." She headed for the kitchen, then stopped in the doorway and turned back, taking in the scene. The colonel and his soldiers, complete camaraderie.

Flynn was a natural leader and these young men depended on him, respected him, revered him. For Flynn not to return to the army would be a sin.

Most important, he'd be miserable. It would be as if she could no longer practice medicine. She'd wither away. She didn't want that for Flynn. No matter how much she liked having him in her life, his staying was completely out of the question.

Chapter Ten

Flynn opened the side door to the house and slogged his way inside. He'd been doing this for two weeks now and damn near killing himself in the process. He couldn't stop for beers at the Cut Loose because the boys rode their bikes with him while he ran. He couldn't smoke unless he did it behind BJ's compost pile after the boys were in bed, and when he did, the smell of burning tobacco and rotting leaves was enough to gag a maggot. What a way to give up cigarettes! What a way to get in shape.

Flo glanced up from her desk. "Ridden hard and put away wet is what you look like, Colonel. Think you might be pushing it a bit?"

"Maybe," he panted. He leaned on her desk, bracing himself on his arms, his head drooping as his breathing returned to normal.

"The doc's got a few more patients, then she's through. The boys beat you back and took off to Margaret's."

Flynn nodded, his heart rate slowing as Flo grinned

and leaned back in her chair. "I'm thinking there's more to your exercising than exercising. Maybe you should be holding back some of that fired-up energy you got for the nighttime, when things are less hectic around here and two little boys are sound asleep and BJ isn't. If you were doing more of what a husband's supposed to be doing at night I'm betting you wouldn't be doing what you're doing now, if you get my drift."

"It's not a drift, Flo. It's a damn avalanche." *And he wished like hell he could do exactly what she suggested.*

But he couldn't. That was the agreement. What BJ wanted and he'd agreed to, sort of. No impromptu sex, no whisking her into the bathroom or anywhere else and having his way with her. They weren't really married. He thought of the boys, the laundry, the chaotic house. That part sure as hell felt married…and he liked it. He felt settled—something new for Flynn MacIntire.

He gave Flo a little salute, made his way upstairs past BJ's bedroom, where he kept their clothes. He wasn't ready to face her room right now, her things by his, reminding him where he wanted to be, with her, holding her, having voracious sex with her. *Right now he'd settle for any kind of sex with her.* Was it possible to be this frustrated and live? Obviously so!

If he went in that room right now he'd lose what control he had and go back downstairs and take BJ in one of her own examining rooms, not caring a rat's ass that she had patients.

He headed for the library, sat on the Oriental rug and massaged his leg. It felt better when BJ did it, but that led to complications on the countertop. Sounded like a

bad movie, and just thinking about it made him horn-
ier still. Was that possible?

Hell, everything BJ did made him horny. Talking to
her, watching her cook or in her little white coat with
her hair pinned on top of her head. All those things
made him want to back her against the nearest wall,
undo her braids and put himself deep inside her.

His body hardened at the thought. He usually tried
to replace such a thought with pain, like fifty push-ups.
He'd done more damn push-ups in the past fourteen
days than he had in all of basic training. He had to get
back to the army, put BJ behind him. He couldn't keep
this regime up and stay sane.

He massaged his leg more, loosening his muscles,
then grabbed a quick shower and went downstairs for
a beer. As he turned the corner into the kitchen, he
caught sight of BJ passing from one examining room
to the other and instantly wanted her. Ah, hell.

He dropped to the floor and started push-ups as Drew
and Petey ran in. Petey climbed on Flynn's back. "It's
my turn to ride Flynn."

Drew pushed at Petey. "It's my turn."

Flynn looked up. "Hey."

Drew stepped away. "Yeah, it's Petey's turn. We
came home to get changed. Grandma Fairmont's taking us to the Schnitzer's bar in Billings. She said it's
neat. She bought us suits to wear, and it has great food
there and we dance. I don't know how to dance, but
she's going to teach me, and we bring presents and
wear little hats."

"To a bar? You guys aren't old enough."

"What the heck are you doing?" Jack said.

Flynn huffed as he pumped up and down. "Don't ask."

Jack chuckled. "I think I know. Heck, I think I've done it. There is another solution, you realize."

"Yeah, and it ain't happening around here."

"I'll get us some beers."

Flynn did more push-ups, trying not to consider that other solution, till he caught sight of BJ's ankle as she walked in. He concentrated on his push-ups, and suddenly saw himself in this position over BJ, pumping into her and...

Piss, he said to himself because there were kids around. All the push-ups in the world wouldn't cure his condition unless BJ was personally involved. He collapsed onto the floor in a heap.

"Get up horsey. Get up," Petey bounced up and down on his back.

"Hi, Jack," said BJ. "What are you doing, Flynn?" she inquired, pulling Petey off him and revving him from horny to desperate just at the sound of her voice. He couldn't get up now. He had a hard-on the size of a fence post.

Jack toed Flynn's leg. "He's recuperating."

"In the middle of the kitchen floor?" BJ said. "Boys, you have to get cleaned up."

Flynn raised his head. "They're going to a bar?"

"Bar mitzvah, in Billings. Grandma Mac's going, too. Mother traded in her Lincoln Town Car and bought a new minivan."

For a second, Flynn wished it were a real bar. Behaving wouldn't be quite so important. "I'm trying to picture Margaret behind the wheel of a minivan. It's not computing."

"It's red. The boys picked it out. She wouldn't even let me have a red bike when I was ten because it was too flashy. I should have been a grandchild."

Flynn grinned as he drew himself up slowly, hoping his body cooperated. "I'll mind the boys. You still have patients."

BJ nodded, tired and grateful. She left, and Flynn sat Petey on one leg and motioned for Drew to sit on the other. "You're taking your grandmothers out tonight and you are to be perfect gentlemen. You're to help them and be their escorts for the evening like—"

"Soldiers all dressed up in their uniforms," Drew added.

"Yes, just like that. Make them proud of you, and you can be proud of yourselves. I'm depending on you boys to mind your manners and be polite." He glanced from one to the other. "Can you do that?"

Drew and Petey stood. "Yes, sir," Drew said, echoed by Petey.

"Good. Now, get a shower and keep the water in the tub this time." They turned for the hallway, and Flynn stood and snagged the beer from Jack. "This is God's way of getting back at me for all the hell I put my dad through."

Jack held his longneck in salutation. "To fatherhood. You're a natural."

Flynn sat on the other stool. "Fatherhood? I have no idea what the hell I'm doing."

"I got news for you—nobody does. You do your best, love your kids and pray it all works out. Not that I'm any expert. I missed most of Ben's youth and I regret that a hell of a lot. It's one of those things that if I could go back and change, I would. But Maggie and I are getting remarried next month. We'll be a family again, though I can never get back the years I lost by staying in Chicago. I loved my job and hated not being with my son. No easy answers."

He eyed Flynn. "Something to think about in those wee hours of the morning when you're lying on the couch, wondering why the hell you're there instead of upstairs."

Flynn drank the beer. "Maybe it will help me forget why I *want* to be upstairs."

"There's only one cure for that and it isn't mental. How's BJ going to manage when you head back to the army? She's looking worn out already. Are you two staying married?"

"Hell, Jack, I…I don't know." He surprised himself with that answer. "I figured BJ and I would divorce sometime, but now we have the boys and leaving her with all this to face alone doesn't seem right, either."

"And you're doing push-ups in the kitchen."

"There is that."

"And I thought *my* life was complicated. You got me beat by a mile." He tapped his bottle against Flynn's. "Good luck." He took a drink. "But I didn't come here to preach. Roy got a speeder over last night and the guy mentioned passing three trucks on the back roads by Cabin Springs."

Flynn's eyes widened. "What the hell's going on?"

"I've been checking around. Sheriff over in Rocky Fork said some folks saw three trucks, one bigger, two smaller, at a roadside pull-off in the mountains. I've been in touch with some of my friends in the Chicago PD. Bogus designer goods are a huge business. Not just women's purses, but perfume, jewelry, baby food, meds, sports equipment—you name it. I'm calling the FBI today to get their take on our little blue wallet. Just thought I'd let you know, since Drew's present to Margaret is what really set this all in motion."

Jack finished the last of his beer and put the bottle in the sink. "Keep this to yourself. Don't need half the town running around with rifles drawn. Drew didn't say anything about what the guys looked like, did he?"

"He's forgotten all about it," Flynn said. "At least, he never mentions it. Been kind of crazy around here."

"The adoption's going okay?"

"Katie and her boyfriend are moving to Billings. It's only an hour away and she'll visit, I'm sure. She's not a bad person. Just had too much responsibility too fast."

Jack headed down the hall and Flynn went to get the boys dressed for the bar mitzvah. How *was* BJ going to handle all this when he left? He'd get home every few months unless he got shipped out. Then it would be a year or longer. Grandma Mac would help and Margaret was a trooper, but he wouldn't be there.

His heart tightened. He couldn't imagine how much the boys would change in a year. That was what all soldiers faced, one of the reasons he'd never married.

He'd married the U.S. Army, instead, and never regretted it…till now.

BJ GLANCED AT THE FILES for tomorrow's patients, then caught sight of Flynn walking down the hall toward the stairs. She breathed a sigh of relief. He'd get the boys ready for the bar mitzvah and remind them about being little gentlemen. Then the relief turned to agony. Broad back, trim waist, great butt—really great butt—hair, or whatever you called a month's growth of fuzz. She didn't care. In fact, she liked it. She liked him, every delicious glorious inch of him.

Had it been two weeks since they'd hidden in the bathroom and had sex? Seemed more like a year…or two.

She bit her lower lip as she continued to watch him. Heat waves pulsed through her, settling in some deep spot inside that wanted a heck of a lot more than heat waves. She felt achy, tense, hungry…very, very hungry.

"That is some hunk of man you got there," said Dixie from behind.

BJ smiled at her friend. "What man?"

Dixie rolled her eyes. "The sexy-as-hell one, the one you just stripped buck naked with your eyes, nearly tackled in the hallway and had carnal knowledge with on the spot. The one you're married to."

"Oh, that man."

Dixie shifted her weight to one leg and folded her arms. "Yeah, that one." She peered at BJ. "You're sort of run-down. Bet I know something, and somebody, that can pump you right up? Having the boys around putting a crimp in your *social life?*"

"There is no *social life*. Remember, this isn't a—"

"Real marriage. So you keep saying, and I keep hoping you're wrong, because from what I've seen it sure seems real to me. No arguing between you two and a lot more *heat*. If there was any more heat this place would combust."

"Flynn's leaving Whistlers Bend, Dixie. He's not staying and I can't ask him to." She waved her hand through the air. "The past two weeks this place is more like LAX than romance central, so you can forget all about heat."

"You didn't." Dixie put on her sassy grin. "My guess is you love him. Why else would you even *think* about asking him to hang around? When are you going to admit it?"

"Okay, okay, what if I do love him? It's one-sided, and that amounts to nothing. The man loves the army. That's his life. Always has been, always will be. I would never ask him to change. He wouldn't be happy." BJ gave her a toothy grin she hoped didn't appear too fake. "And that's just fine with me. I got the boys. What more do I need?"

"Sex."

Kean tapped on the window. "Hi, Doc, Dixie."

If he'd heard the *sex* comment she'd die. Instead, Kean said to BJ, "We almost have the design for the addition finished. I'm here to double-check measurements. When you get a chance, can you tell me about that swing set you want for the boys, and where we should build it, and if you and Flynn aren't having sex you're both idiots?"

BJ exchanged *oh, hell* looks with Dixie as Kean left and Flynn and the boys trotted down the hallway from the upstairs.

Flynn greeted Dixie, then said to BJ, "I'm taking the boys to your mother's now."

"Tell her to call if there are any problems." She studied the boys and beamed. "Oh, my, you're both so handsome in your new suits. Petey, no cake or candy. I don't care how good you think it is. Grandma Fairmont can take care of you."

She kissed the boys, then Flynn clapped their hands and made for the door. She glanced back to Dixie. "You seem worried, kind of pale and concerned. Are you okay?"

Dixie brightened, though the smile seemed forced. She twitched her hips and fluffed her bob. "Are you kidding? I'm hot and sexy as always. Just ask the boys at the café. I'm keeping them on their toes. You know me—never a sick day in my life. Just thought I'd stop over before my evening shift at the Sage and see how you were holding up. You and Flynn come by for dinner." She winked. "Unless you have other plans for your evening alone. Wine, Brie, thee."

"There is no *thee!*"

"There sure was a thee weeks ago."

"Well, not now."

Dixie left and BJ showed Kean where to put the wooden swing and how she wanted the addition connected to the main house, with a glassed-in breezeway instead of just a walkway. She also wanted more windows across the back so she could keep an eye on the boys playing, and maybe a tree house in the big oak by the compost pile.

After Kean left without further reference to her sex life, thank heavens, she went back inside, drained to the core, and sat at the counter by the window. Tea might help her feel better. Herbal. The thought of caffeine made her insides crawl. She nuked a cup, drank half and felt sick. She headed upstairs for the bathroom and promptly lost it and the crackers she'd eaten earlier.

"BJ," Flynn said, "what's wrong?"

"Nothing. I'm fine."

"Kneeling in the bathroom is a new hobby?" He handed her a wet towel and glass of water.

"Just ate something that didn't agree with me." She sat on the edge of the tub, took a mint from her pocket and put it in her mouth, the flavor settling her stomach a bit.

"Want to tell me what's really going on here, or do I have to play Twenty Questions and drive us both nuts?"

"I'm sick. I'll be fine."

"When? You wouldn't be carrying around mints in your pocket if this was the first time you'd gotten like this."

She put her elbow on her knees, rested her chin in her palm and gazed at Flynn. "You're going to harass the heck out of me unless I tell you, so I might as well get this over with. I don't know what's going on. No fever, no swelling anywhere, no apparent infections. I eat and I get sick. It comes in waves. I'm okay, then not okay, and I feel like a big truck ran over me. I'd say I was pregnant, but I know that's impossible.

She gave him a sad smile. "Funny, isn't it, the doc can't diagnose her own ailments."

"Nothing funny about being sick. You've seemed tired, but I chalked it up to all that's going on. I should have paid more attention."

"I told myself it's nerves, tension, new-mother-itus, except I'm getting worse, not better, even though we're settling into somewhat of a routine." She sipped the water.

"What if something's wrong, Flynn? Really wrong, and I'm truly sick? And now I have Petey and Drew to care for." She raked her fingers through her hair, worry making her feel worse than ever. "Who's going to care for the boys, if the prognosis is…?"

She couldn't finish as a huge lump lodged in her throat. He hunkered down in front of her, took the wet towel from her hand and gently wiped her face, then tucked a stray strand of hair behind her ear. "Don't cry on me, Doc. You can yell and argue and throw a holy fit, but don't cry. You're about the bravest person I've ever met, and if you cry you're going to scare the hell out of me because I don't know how to make it right."

She touched his cheek, his chin smooth from a fresh shave, his eyes wise and kind. His face was more handsome than any man's on earth should be. "I don't feel brave. I just feel afraid, out of control."

"I'm here and you're allowed to be afraid. Whatever it is, we'll see it through together. You're not alone. You have your mother, who's incredible with the boys, and Flo pitches in, and Grandma Mac will always be there. And you have me. *We* can *handle* it. I'm not the kind of guy who runs when things get tough—you can bank on that. I'll get an extended leave."

"I think you've extended your leave as far as it will go. You're due to go before an army medical board so they can certify you *fit for duty*." She smiled at him, grateful and appreciative. "Whoever thought we'd be having a conversation like this?"

He cracked a smile. "It's a long way from you putting oatmeal in my helmet. I'm taking you into Billings, to the hospital." He put his arm around her shoulders, then under her legs, and hoisted her into his arms as if she were a rag doll.

She stared at him wide eyed, holding on to his neck and shoulders for support, amazed how good, how comforted she felt to be here, to have someone else with her. "I'm not dead yet. I can walk. And I should get my jacket and purse."

"I'm sure they have your name on file at the hospital, and my jacket's in the car." He made for the stairs. "Relax—it'll calm your stomach."

"Guess this means I can't drive."

"Doc, I've had enough of your driving to last a lifetime." He trotted down the steps—something he hadn't been close to doing two weeks ago.

"You're just jealous because I'm a better driver than you are."

He laughed. "Sure you are. Keep telling yourself that if it makes you feel good."

She laid her head on his shoulder, beyond tired. As Flynn had said, whatever happened she wasn't alone. He was with her, and somehow that made all the difference in the world.

FLYNN PACED in the hospital waiting room. He checked his watch again and swallowed a growl. That nurse who'd brought him here had exactly two minutes to get back to him, or he was finding BJ on his own if he had to tear the whole damn hospital apart to do it. Why in the hell he had to leave while they helped her into a gown was beyond him. He was her husband, dammit. He'd seen it all and then some.

"Mr. MacIntire," the nurse said, "if you follow me I'll take you to your wife."

When she opened the curtain for him he saw BJ sitting on the edge of the cot in one of those stupid gowns, bug-eyed and totally stunned. His insides froze. *Dear God, what if he lost BJ?*

"Flynn?" She sounded groggy, as if waking from a dream.

He took her hand. "Whatever it is, we'll see this through together, I swear."

"I believe that now more than ever." She covered his hand with her other one and scooted over on the cot. "You should sit down."

"That bad?"

"Wouldn't jump right to bad." She motioned beside her. "Sure you don't want to sit?"

"For God's sake, BJ, just tell me. I can take it. Whatever it is I've been through worse."

"It's not exactly worse. It's closer to different or maybe mysterious or—"

"BJ!"

She held his hands tight. "You're going to be a father. You already *are* with Drew and Petey, but—"

"You're…pregnant?" He sat down on the cot next to her, his head spinning. He opened his mouth to say something. Speech, though, was impossible. Finally, he managed, "I…I thought you getting pregnant was out of the question."

She shrugged. "Well, we got married so I could have a baby, but I didn't plan on this."

"So, how did it?" He closed his eyes for a moment to get a grip. "I know how but…how?"

"At my age hormones go a little wacky, can overproduce and… My med-school prof called it *the last fling of the ovary*. Not too technical, but tells it like it is." She stared at Flynn. "I'm not the first woman to get unexpectedly pregnant for the first time at forty or even later."

"This is some last fling. I was thinking more like Corvette or Ducati or climbing Everest." He shook his head to see if he was dreaming. He wasn't. "Baby?"

She leveled him a hard look. "You don't have to say it like it's the curse from the Black Lagoon."

"But a baby?"

"No, I'm having a teenager."

He swallowed. "It's a bit of a shock. I hadn't counted on fathering a child at this stage of my life. Hell, I hadn't counted on it, period. Doesn't exactly fit in with—"

She stood in front of him and glared. "Well, we wouldn't want to inconvenience the mighty Colonel MacIntire and not have something fit in with his life, now, would we?"

"I didn't mean it that way."

She peered at him through lowered lids. "Yes, you did. You just said so. But don't worry about a thing. The baby and I and the boys will manage quite well without you. In fact, we'll be flipping terrific."

She whipped the curtain back, nearly tearing it from the rod, then pointed a stiff finger down the hallway. "Out."

"I'm not leaving you," he said as a nurse came by and told them to keep it down.

"Yes, you are," BJ insisted, not keeping it down at all and jabbing her finger again. "Because I'm surely not riding with you. You might be *inconvenienced.*"

"This is taking a little getting used to, that's all."

"Don't bother. I'll call Mother. She's in town and can pick me up."

Flynn slid off the cot. "You're upset. Probably a hormone thing."

"Keep talking like that and you'll be a dead thing."

"I'll care for the baby. Settle down, okay? I can certainly afford to do—"

"Money?" Her voice rose to nearly a screech and the nurse was back with another warning. BJ ignored her and continued. "You're concerned about the money?"

"No, no. Bad choice of word." He held up his hands in defense. He'd been in firefights that were less problematic than this. "I don't mind a baby, BJ."

The nurse shook her head at him. "How long you been married?"

"Not long enough," he said.

"I've wanted a baby for fifteen years," BJ snarled. "Fifteen. Would have married the cretin from hell just to have a baby. You don't have to *mind* anything, Colonel Flynn MacIntire."

She pulled herself up tall, her nipples poking through the gown, making him remember better times. *But they sure weren't better now.*

"We're getting a divorce, and the sooner the better. The boys will have to deal. You being all pissy over this pregnancy isn't good for them or me."

"You're being melodramatic, blowing what I said way out of proportion."

"I'll raise the children, and you don't have to trouble yourself one bit."

"You tell him, girl," the nurse encouraged as she passed again.

"Thanks a lot," Flynn said to the nurse, then said to BJ, "I was shocked all to hell and back. I didn't choose my words wisely. The baby's—"

"Out!" BJ jabbed her finger one more time.

"Be reasonable. I can drive you—"

"You can drive me *nowhere*. I'll get to Whistlers Bend on my own—"

"I'll call you a cab," the nurse offered in a huff.

BJ ignored her. "And you can move back to the MacIntire home, the army or straight to hell, but you are not planting your sorry, I-don't-want-to-be-inconvenienced butt in my house again."

Flynn put his hands to his hip, furrowed his brow and lowered his voice. "I apologize for not being more supportive. Having a baby is fine, and I'll sleep where I want and when I want. You came here with me—you're leaving with me. I'm taking care of you, I'm taking care of our baby and the boys, and that's the end of this discussion."

She tossed her head, her golden hair flying. "Is that an order, Colonel?"

"You bet your sweet ass it is." He glared at the nurse. Then he flipped his jacket around BJ, covering her backside, and scooped her up into his arms.

"Put me down!"

"As soon as we get to the car." He strode toward the exit, the people in the lobby parting like the Red Sea.

"What about her clothes?" the nurse asked.

"Mail 'em."

"Should I phone security?"

"No." BJ folded her arms and stared straight ahead. "The Bear is in a mood and it's best not to poke him."

"Good call, Fairmont," Flynn said as he kicked open the door.

"I'll get you for this, MacIntire."

"I'm sure you will, but right now we do things *my* way."

Chapter Eleven

An hour later, as she sat in the passenger seat next to Flynn, BJ was still seething. She really was a much better driver. How could he not see that? He rounded the corner to her house and slowed. "Holy hell," he said. "The place is lit up like the electricity company just moved in. What in the world is going on this time?"

BJ bolted up. "Petey?"

"I have my cell. Someone would have contacted us."

Before Flynn came to a complete stop, she opened the car door and ran up the garden walkway to the house, Flynn in hot pursuit behind her. She went in and tore down the hall—and spotted Dixie and Maggie at the kitchen table, drinking from mugs.

"What's going on?" BJ panted.

They looked at each other, then BJ, and raised their eyebrows. Maggie said, "You're dressed in a hospital gown, barefoot and in Flynn's army jacket and you're asking *us* what's going on?"

She grabbed the jacket closed around her. "Where are the boys?"

"Upstairs. Both fine," Maggie said. "They're packing," Dixie added. "Margaret's helping. You and Flynn better sit down."

"I'm beginning to really hate that suggestion," he said. He studied Maggie. "Why is there an iron skillet in front of you?" He eyed Dixie. "Is that a camouflage shirt and pants you have on?"

Dixie fluffed her collar and batted her eyes. "You know I always dress for the occasion." Maggie picked up the skillet and tested the feel in one hand, then the other. "Chased Jack around the kitchen with it once."

BJ braced her arms on the table. "If I don't get answers in one second I'll be the one chasing with the frying pan."

Maggie glanced at Flynn. "Has she been like this all night?"

Flynn sighed. "You have no idea."

Maggie said, "Two strangers at the diner were asking about a little boy, seven or eight, with brown hair and brown eyes, who likes to play at the old depot. They must have realized Dixie was onto them, because they ran off before Jack showed up. We thought it best to tell Margaret what was going on, and Jack sent Roy to get her and the boys in Billings. Jack suggested taking the boys out of town till this was over, though we're really not sure what *this* is."

Dixie knocked Maggie's pan with her knuckles. "Jack and Roy are casing the area, so we're on guard duty. Your mother's taking the boys to Martha's Vineyard—flying out tomorrow afternoon. One of her friends has a summer home on the island."

BJ groused, "And no one bothered to call either Flynn or me with this tidbit of info because…?"

Dixie winked. "Hey, we got it covered." She smirked. "And you barely do," she said on a giggle. "And we figured you and Flynn had gone out for a little *quality time.* Don't suppose you want to tell us about this quality-time gown you're sporting? A little dress-up? I got to tell you there are much better outfits out there. You can borrow my French maid's outfit."

BJ, Maggie and Flynn stared at Dixie. "Fr-French maid?" Maggie stammered. "How do you know?"

Margaret came into the kitchen. "Hello, my de—" She stopped dead and stared at her daughter. "Barbara Jean? Have you completely lost your mind? Why are you dressed like…like *that?*"

A wicked gleam suddenly brightened her green eyes, an expression BJ had never seen on her completely proper mother before. "Wanting something a little out of the ordinary, perhaps? Oh, my, marriage *can* be fun. How I miss those times," she said on a sigh. "Next time you should consider a French maid's outfit."

BJ huffed, "Is the whole world sex crazy?"

Margaret shrugged. "Some people think money rules the world. They're wrong, dear. It's sex. I should have told you."

"Flynn, BJ," Drew called. His and Petey's footsteps clambered down the hall. The boys tumbled into the kitchen. "Grandma Fairmont's taking us to visit Louis and see the Yankees and eat peanuts and hot dogs."

Petey spread his arms wide and made engine sounds as he glided around the kitchen. "We're going to fly on a big airplane and eat pretzels out of little bags." He stopped when he got to BJ, and his eyes grew large. "Why are you dressed in Flynn's jacket again? It's not Halloween, is it?"

She kissed Petey's head and hunkered down beside Drew, thankful Flynn's jacket fell below her behind. "Can you do something for me, something very important? I want you to think about the day you ran away."

"Do I have to? I don't want to think about that. I want to think about the ocean and seeing the Yankees."

Flynn squatted beside her. "This will help Sheriff Jack."

Drew pulled himself up straight. "It's my duty to help the sheriff, even if I don't want to, is that right?"

Flynn nodded. "Tell us again about the trucks and the depot. Did the drivers see you?"

Drew bit his bottom lip. "Maybe."

BJ felt every bone in her body go to jelly. "We're not mad that you ran away. It's all over with now. You have to tell us what you saw."

"I didn't tell you before 'cause I didn't want you to be mad and not adopt me and Petey. The men saw me, but I ran and hid in the cave. They didn't find me 'cause they didn't know where to look, and they were in a big hurry and said they'd come back later. I didn't see what they were doing 'cause I was hiding. I was afraid."

Flynn mussed Drew's hair. "That was real good, Drew. You did great. And you don't have to be afraid anymore because we're all here to take care of you."

Margaret said to Flynn, a trace of concern in her voice, "And now that you're here we can leave homeland security in your most capable military hands, for which I am terribly grateful." She patted his arm.

Flynn said to her, "I'll drive you and the boys to the airport in Billings just to make sure everything's okay."

She eyed her daughter. "Not BJ?"

"I have office hours."

Margaret winked at Flynn.

"Hey," BJ said. "I saw that."

"I'll tuck the boys in," Flynn said as he corralled them toward the stairs.

"I'll walk you out." BJ headed toward the door and Margaret quirked her left eyebrow. "In that attire? An army jacket and bare legs?"

"It's dark, Mother. No one will see, and if they do it will give them all something to gossip over."

Margaret sighed. "Since you and Flynn married, this town has enough gossip to keep it churning for a very long time. Must we add more?"

Dixie chuckled. "I should do a column in the *Whistle Stop* on what you all are up to over here. Always wanted to be a reporter."

"Oh, no, you don't." BJ shook her head. "What would the Sage and all of us do without you to get us food?" She hooked her arm through her mother's and Dixie's. Maggie handed Dixie the skillet, snagged her crutches and followed her out into the garden. BJ stopped by the little fountain, the moon reflecting in the still water, a gazillion stars overhead.

"I'm not making the same mistake I did about the wedding. I'm pregnant. Barely, but pregnant all the same."

Margaret gasped, then laughed, "Well, it's about time. I couldn't be happier."

Dixie clapped her hands. "Finally, you'll be fatter than me. I am *so* looking forward to this."

Maggie sucked in a deep breath. "Holy cow, what does Flynn have to say?"

"He's less than thrilled."

Margaret hugged BJ. "He'll come around, dear. The good ones always do, and Flynn MacIntire is indeed one of those. He's just a little concerned over all that's happened. He has a lot of responsibility now. A wife and three kids in less than a month? That's enough to send any man running for the hills. But Flynn didn't, did he. In fact, he's upstairs tucking two of those reasons into bed as we speak." She laughed. "He reminds me of your father in a lot of ways. Good to have a man around again."

BJ knew she must look as if she'd been shot from a cannon. "You're right. I haven't been fair to Flynn. I kind of went a little crazy at the hospital. I don't know what I was thinking."

Margaret gave her a mother's smile. "You're thinking *everyone's* been waiting to get pregnant for years and years. Believe me, they haven't. Especially an army colonel. Patch things up. You have children to consider who really love Flynn. He's a keeper."

Margaret kissed her, she shared hugs with Dixie and Maggie, then watched them walk down the garden path toward the gate that would soon be gone.

And that was okay. She'd gotten what she'd wanted and so much more. Flynn hadn't. He'd gotten pretty well screwed in the deal. She grinned. Actually, she'd been the one who'd gotten well screwed.

Flynn hadn't wanted any of this. He wanted back in the army. She owed him an apology. *and, most important, she owed him a way out of all this.*

She went back into the kitchen and found Flynn in front of the open fridge. She scurried on by, checked on the boys, who were already asleep, then changed into her pink sweatsuit. She tugged out the top part and gazed in the mirror. Barbara Jean Fairmont pregnant. How great was that?

Plenty great. And that Flynn was the father made her happier than she'd ever dreamed. What a gene pool! The past two weeks of them all together had been hectic, but a good hectic—at least in her book. And now it was over and she had to let Flynn go; it was time for him to move on.

Her heart suddenly felt as though someone had squeezed the life right out of it, and she sat on the edge of the bed. She picked up Flynn's jacket that she'd just taken off and inhaled the inside, inhaling Flynn, then held his field jacket tight to her and buried her face in the soft material.

She'd miss him. She'd miss his common sense and determination, and his sparring with her and teasing her about her driving.

No one got to her like Flynn…on more levels than one. She'd miss feeling safe and secure with him. She'd miss his laundry in with hers, his dishes in with hers, and she'd sure miss the sex.

Except it was more than sex. They'd made love,

wonderful meaningful love. Sex was taking what you wanted with no regard for the partner. Neither of them did that.

God, she loved him. From the bottom of her soul and deep in her heart, she loved this man she'd shared so much with and who'd shared so much of himself with her.

She put down his jacket and forbade herself to cry over losing him. She'd had him for a little while and she had his baby. That was more than she'd ever thought possible. She went down to the kitchen. He'd set two places at the table, and chicken soup simmered on the stove—the smell of home. Things wouldn't be the same when Flynn left.

But if he stayed he wouldn't be the man she knew and admired and loved. He'd change. She never wanted him to change. As much as she hated it, as much as she didn't want to, she had to get rid of Flynn MacIntire!

Good grief. That was how she'd gotten into this!

She squared her shoulders and prepared for battle. With his baby on the way, getting rid of him would be a battle and a half. Well, she might not be a tank commander, but she intended to win. She had to for his sake.

"Smells great," she said as she walked in with a big smile. "You cook around here as much as I do."

"Except I have no idea what pregnant women eat, so I winged it." He had a towel around his middle and a concerned glint in his eyes as he set a plate of sandwiches on the table.

"Pretzels are good."

"The nutritional value of salted wood. Can you tolerate sliced turkey on plain bread, no condiments, and chicken soup from a package, no fat? It's all I could come up with from what we have in the pantry."

We. She loved the sound of *we.*

"How about Peeps? Peeps are in the pantry. I have purple ones left."

He leveled her a get-real look.

"Right. Peeps for dessert. Sandwich and soup for now. Thanks for rounding up some food—I'm starved."

She sat across from him and planned her attack. She needed to smooth the waters before she stirred them up again.

"I want you to believe that I'm sorry I was such a pain at the hospital. I just imagine everyone's supposed to be as wild as I am over this baby. But I can understand why you're not. This isn't your dream—it's mine. Since the boys have gone with Mother, this will give us a perfect opportunity to set the divorce in motion and get you back in the army. That was the agreement."

He stared at her as if she'd sprouted another head. Guess she shouldn't have fired all her guns at once. "You're pregnant with my child. When the boys are adopted *my* name will be on that form, too. You can forget divorce."

She shook her head. "I got you into this kid situation. It wasn't your choosing. The marriage has *I trapped Flynn MacIntire* stamped all over it and that's no marriage at all. We said we'd divorce when I got the baby." She held up her hands. "Ta-da. Baby!"

Flynn leaned across the table, eyes steely, jaw set,

and stage-whispered through clenched teeth, "And I'm just supposed to walk away from my child?"

"I'm putting on an addition. I'm the town doctor. Our child will be here anytime you want to show up. I have phone, fax, e-mail. There's no reason not to carry out the original plan and you leave. You can always come back." She dug into the soup. "Gee, this is really good."

He sat perfectly still, then finally said, "I get no voice in this?"

She shook her head. "You already did about a month ago when all this started and the arrangement was to divorce."

He picked up a sandwich. "I'm not divorcing you, BJ."

"Being in a trapped marriage is what you want? Oh, that's a great way to raise kids. You'll resent me, resent them and resent us. Because there should be no us."

She bit into her sandwich and sat back and looked at him. "You're free, Flynn. You get what you want, the army, and I get what I want, children. No one loses. We all win. Your soup's getting cold."

"I don't give a flying fig about the soup, but nothing about this is honorable."

"You can't marry out of honor. It takes more than that these days. It won't work for either of us and there's no reason you have to be around all the time to raise our child. I have an incredible support group. I'm financially well-off, intelligent. I'm older—not some twenty-something twit who goes wacko over the sniffles. I got the kids and my life covered. Go."

"And I'm the sperm donor."

She rolled her shoulders. "Well, you're a very good sperm donor. Handsome, smart, brave. You like sports, but everyone has some flaws."

His eyes got beady; steam curled from his head. "You really believe you can do it all."

"I'm a woman of the twenty-first century. Of course I can do it all. And I'll get help."

He stood and glared. "And you don't need me."

She chewed on her bottom lip, then brightened. "Hey, you make a really great sandwich."

Chapter Twelve

He put his palms flat on the table, braced his arms and leaned her way. "I'm going to the Cut Loose and have a beer with the other sperm donors. This isn't over, Doc, but arguing with a pregnant woman isn't good for you or the baby. You need to know the divorce won't happen."

"What if I just file?"

"On what grounds?"

"I don't know—I'm not a lawyer. But there's got to be something out there. Irreconcilable driving differences sounds good."

He rounded the table, brought his hungry lips to hers and kissed her…and she kissed him back, because when it came to Flynn MacIntire, she was nothing but a slut and good intentions went right out the window.

How could she insist on divorce one minute and lap up his kisses the next?

His smoldering blue eyes met hers. "That is not the kiss of a woman wanting a divorce."

"So I'm in it for the sex?"

"Sex works. And we have children."

"Not enough. Not for me." It was time to end this episode in her life and quit playing around. The mature, logical, intelligent way to end this was honesty.

She put down her sandwich, stood and looked him in the eyes. "Okay, here it is, the truth. No more games or smart-ass cracks. I love you—have since high school—and our month together was the best month of my life. But none of this matters because you don't love me—you love the army. That's not a criticism or a complaint. It's a fact. I can live with it, but I cannot stay married to you, because of it. *That* would not be honorable. I don't want to live a lie, Flynn, and neither do you. This is over. We're over as a couple."

She kissed him on the cheek, aware of the stunned expression on his face, and continued. "You know I'm right. This will all work out because we're friends, very good friends, and we're intelligent mature responsible adults who will do whatever it takes to raise happy healthy, well-adjusted children."

She added, "Well, I'm glad that's over. Now, you can go have your beer and I'm getting a shower and then off to bed. The boys will be up at the crack of dawn, bursting with excitement and more energy than I've ever had in my life."

She walked into the hall, leaving Flynn alone in the kitchen. She felt relieved, but also more depressed than she'd ever had been. Not exactly the perfect ending to their nonmarriage, but an end nonetheless, and that was what really mattered.

THE NEXT MORNING BJ waved to the boys, Margaret and Flynn as they drove off in Margaret's minivan. Never had she expected to see Flynn MacIntire behind the wheel of a minivan. It didn't seem to bother him, but it sure shocked the heck out of her. They hadn't talked since last night, and that was good. Everything was settled. She'd get over him. Actually, she wouldn't. She'd just learn to live without him.

"Call me," she yelled after them, and waved again to the boys. She hated to see them go, but their leaving was the safest thing to do. Flynn tooted the horn and waved back as she watched the van round the corner onto Main. *What a morning.*

She went back inside and rifled through her files. Flo came in and stopped dead. BJ could feel her stare boring into her back. "If you start doing the office work around here, guess I'll have to take over doctoring."

"What did I do with Flynn's file? I had it out last night. I was working on it, and now I don't know what in the world I did with it."

Flo snagged it off the desktop and held it out. "You mean *this* file?"

"I've got pregnancy meltdown."

"Honey, what you got is Flynn MacIntire meltdown. I'm suspecting you've had it for years and years and it's getting worse and worse."

BJ opened the file and pulled out her notes. "Last night I told him I loved him and I wanted a divorce, and now I'm going to make him want it as much as I do."

"You love him and you want a divorce. Gee, that

makes sense." She nodded at the chair behind the desk. "Maybe you should sit down."

"I'm fine."

"All I know is you and Flynn got a baby on the way, and that man's going to stay married to you for that reason alone unless you take up with somebody else—and I sure can't see that happening."

"Not me, but what about Flynn. What if *he* takes up with someone?" She closed the file and held it up. "Like the U.S. army. "

"Can't curl up with a tank at the end of the day."

BJ ignored the remark. "I'm going to call Fort Carson and confirm that appointment Flynn has with the medical board to get him authorized *fit for duty*. I'll fly there today, talk to them doctor to doctor and turn over his records so there aren't any glitches. Then I'll tell Flynn he has the appointment, make it sound as if the army instigated it. He'll go, see all those tanks and uniforms and jeeps and military paraphernalia and remember how much he loves it and how he wants his old life back and divorce is the answer."

"You want to divorce Flynn that bad?"

BJ's heart felt like a piece of concrete in her chest. Her shoulders sagged along with her bravado. "I love him. I want him free, Flo. I want him to do what he wants and be the man he's meant to be, and he can't do that with a wife and kids at home and him worrying about us."

"A lot of other couples do it."

She gripped Flo's hand. "Because they love each other and they make their marriage work. Their love is the key. Flynn wants to stay together out of obligation. I don't want to be an obligation. I don't have to be. With help I am more than capable of taking care of myself, my children and this town."

She gestured at her office. "This is my life. I wouldn't want to be trapped in the army. How could I let Flynn be trapped in Whistlers Bend in a doctor's office? Besides, he'll always feel this wasn't his decision so much as something thrust upon him."

She nodded and picked up the phone. "I've given this a lot of thought. It will work."

Flo's mouth dropped. "The trouble is, I think you're right."

FLYNN MADE HIS WAY up the garden path and into the office. He glanced around at the emptiness. "Hey, Flo. Where is everyone? Thought the doc had office hours."

Flo put down the phone. "She did. I had to reschedule them all. Do you know how cranky people get when I reschedule? It's more that they'll miss their turn at gossip ground zero."

Flynn's eyes widened. "BJ's that sick that she can't do appointments?"

"Not exactly." Flo drummed her fingers on the desktop. "I'm supposed to tell you she's at the hospital about a patient, which isn't a lie. But she's not in Billings at the hospital—she's in Fort Carson, Colorado, and the patient is you."

If Flo had smacked him upside the head with a stethoscope he couldn't have been more surprised. "You want to run that by me again?"

"She's on a mission, Colonel. Flew off to meet with the doctors at Fort Carson to help get you reinstated for active duty. Her great plan is you'll realize how much you love the army and divorce her because you don't want to be tied down to a wife and kids."

"She told you that."

"Yep. 'Course, she didn't expect me to tell you, but you have a right to know."

Flo leaned back in her chair and studied him as if she'd caught him in the crosshair of a rifle. "The real question to you, Colonel, is do you want her to get her way? I figure that pretty much depends on if you love her or if you don't."

"Love her? Love her? Ah, damn."

Flo sat up straight, ready to get back to work as usual. "Guess that means she's right and you two divorce."

"I didn't say that."

"Well, I sure as heck didn't hear a pledge of undying love, either."

Flynn held up his hands. "I mean damn that I didn't realize before now that I love her. I thought about this all night and all the way back from the airport. I can't imagine living without BJ. She's my partner, my friend, my—"

"Wife?" Flo gave him a cocky grin.

"Yeah, my wife." He gave her a cocky grin in return. "I don't want to lose her."

He hitched his chin toward the rest of the house. "I don't want to lose all this. The kids, the chaos, the meals together. All of us piling into the car—hopefully with me driving—running off for ice cream or fishing. Ever see BJ bait a hook?" He chuckled. "She's priceless."

"Sounds like true love to me. Getting BJ to put a worm on a hook is something else and you believing she's the best makes it a done deal. Problem is, Colonel MacIntire, you're telling all this good stuff to the wrong gal."

He pulled his wallet from his pocket and slid out a phone number. A small photo fell to the desk.

Flo picked it up. "Whose baby?"

"When BJ wanted to adopt a Third-World child I contacted a missionary I'd become friends with and he sent me the picture. The baby's an orphan, but then we got the boys, and now BJ's pregnant." He took the photo from Flo and stuck it back in his wallet.

"You should tell BJ, Flynn."

"Four kids?" He chuckled. "That's a lot of kids." He dialed.

"You're calling her?"

"The hospital at Fort Carson. I'll have the staff stall a certain doctor till I can get there and straighten things out. I've got to win the battle and the war, and I'm just not sure how to do it."

"You're an army man. You'll figure it out."

He connected with the hospital and pleaded his case, then jogged upstairs. After stuffing sweats and gym shoes into a duffel, he got in his car, got his uniform from Grandma Mac's and headed for the airport. First, he had to pass that damn physical for the medical board. After that, he had to figure out how to make things work between him and BJ. He didn't have a clue. But something would come to him.

BJ STARED AT THE *New England Journal of Medicine*. She'd already read it at her own office, and now she'd darn near memorized it cover to cover at another doctor's office. What could be taking this—she looked at the nameplate on the desk—Dr. Bradford so long? She'd been waiting here for three hours.

He needed to redecorate. What a boring place. Gray and brown everything. Even the picture of the Pentagon on the far wall was gray. Did these people ever hear of teal, mauve, sage, burgundy? Burgundy would be good, and some plants. This room cried out for plants.

A knock came at the door and a pretty, young woman in army clothes came in. "I'm sorry, ma'am. Dr. Bradford has—"

"An emergency. I understand. But perhaps I could speak to another doctor on the fitness board. I won't take much time."

She smiled sweetly, too sweetly. "Having other doctors visit our staff on behalf of a soldier is a bit out of the ordinary, and the board wasn't prepared to see you. Would you care for something to eat?"

BJ nodded. "A plain cheese sandwich would be wonderful, if it's not too much trouble."

"Of course, ma'am. Anything for a friend of the colonel's."

"You know Colonel MacIntire?"

She blushed. "Everybody knows Colonel MacIntire, ma'am." She closed the door behind her.

What the heck did young soldier perky-boobs mean by that? As much as BJ didn't want it to, jealousy crawled up her spine and she felt her eyes get beady and probably turn greener. She said in a juvenile singsong voice, "Everybody knows Colonel MacIntire, ma'am."

"Not everybody," said Flynn from behind her.

She spun around. "For someone so darn big you sure move quiet."

"That's the plan."

Her breath caught. "You're in uniform. You're never in uniform."

"This isn't Whistlers Bend."

He seemed very much in command of the situation. And she'd just interfered in his business. Not good. "What…what are you here for?"

"That's my line."

How was she going to get out of this? What should she tell him? *Think, BJ. Think.* "You'd look much better in blue or a nice turquoise than in this mix of greens and browns and—is that a blob of black on your thigh?"

He arched his very commanding eyebrow. "BJ?"

Busted. "How'd you know I was here?"

"Domestic intel."

"That's army talk for—"

"Flo. She ratted you out."

"Well, that does it. She's fired."

"You can't fire her. You couldn't run the place without her. Are you going to tell me why you're here or not?"

BJ shrugged. "I'm sure domestic intel already told you, so let's not get redundant. But the dear doctors around this establishment seem to be too busy to talk to me so, my great plan was for nothing."

"They were busy."

"Flynn, all doctors are busy. Three hours is a little excessive."

"They were busy with a patient. Me."

She slowly smiled. "Really? Did you do it? Are you *in?*"

"Have to wait for the official word, but I'd say so."

She flung herself into his arms. "Oh, I'm so happy for you. I really am."

She felt his hands slide around her back and hold her tight, as though he meant it, as though he wanted her there. But that was too bad, because as a couple they were over. She held on for a moment longer, remembering him, not quite ready to give him up. Who was she kidding? She'd never be ready. "So, that's it." She gave him a sincere smile. "You're off to some new front, and I'll see you whenever."

"That's not a good plan, Doc."

"Let's not argue. I'm not up to it, okay? You belong right where you are, wearing really bad colors, but you're happy about it, so that's fine. Let's not try to change what's obviously the right thing to do."

"I love you."

"No, you don't. You're just happy because you're back in the army, and you don't want to disappoint me because you know I love you. That's the way you are. Always saving everyone." She touched his cheek. "No need to this time, Colonel MacIntire. I'm already fine."

"I'm not in love with you to make *you* happy. I'm in love with you because it makes *me* happy."

"It'll fade—temporary condition brought on by a

burst of euphoria. I'm sure it has a medical name. I just can't remember it."

"Take two aspirin and I'll be fine?"

"I was thinking more along the lines of a beer with your buddies."

He picked her up at her waist and set her on the edge of the doctor's desk, knocking the nameplate over. "You're going to listen to me, Barbara Jean Fairmont. I love you because you're beautiful and smart and selfless and nurturing and responsible and a whole raft of other things."

"Like, I'm the mother of your child and you can't get beyond that."

He tucked a strand of hair behind her ear. "And I don't want to get beyond it. I'm thrilled you're having our baby, but those aren't the only reasons I love you." His eyes darkened; a soft smile spread across his wonderful lips. "You saved me, BJ. Before we married all I could imagine was war and dying and the battlefield. I couldn't get beyond it. I have other times, but not this time. It haunted me, day and night. Then you came along."

"And I haunted you?"

His smile grew. "Yeah, you haunted me and then you mesmerized me and you charmed me. You're in my life now, and the boys and our home. I'll never forget the men who served with me and especially the ones who lost their lives, but now I have you. I love you. You're the world to me."

She bit her bottom lip, afraid she was dreaming. "Me?"

"You. I want to be with you, always."

She framed his face in her palms. "You're an army man through and through, Flynn. You don't belong in Whistlers Bend any more than I belong here with soldier perky-boobs."

His eyebrows rose. "Who?"

"Not important. What is, is that you can't give up the army. "

"And I'm not. At least, not yet. Fort Harrison in Helena is being reconfigured into an army Combat Training Center. I can't commute from Whistlers Bend, but I can do most weekends and I get leave. You'll see a lot more of me."

"I want this to work and you want this to work, but you've always been on the front lines, Flynn. You've been all over the world. That's what you do. You go off and fight battles and lead men and women to defend our country. I respect that and I don't intend for you to change."

"I'd like more in my life than living out of a duffel bag, BJ."

"You'd like a Ducati."

He grinned. "I want, a home, kids, you." He kissed her. "If you'll have me, boring uniform and all." He reached into his pocket. "Besides, I have Peeps. Can you say no to a man who brings you Peeps?"

She laughed, then cried. "I've dreamed of this."

"We can do this, Doc. We can make this work."

"Colonel Flynn MacIntire, you are a fabulous husband. Together we can do anything."

* * * * *

*Welcome to the world of American Romance!
Turn the page for excerpts from our
November 2005 titles.*

CINDERELLA CHRISTMAS
by Shelley Galloway

BREAKFAST WITH SANTA
by Pamela Browning

HOLIDAY HOMECOMING
by Mary Anne Wilson

*Also, watch for a new anthology,
CHRISTMAS, TEXAS STYLE,
which features three fun and warmhearted holiday
stories by three of your favorite American Romance
authors, Tina Leonard, Leah Vale and Linda Warren.
Let these stories show you what it's like to celebrate
Christmas down on the ranch.*

We hope you'll enjoy every one of these books!

We're thrilled to introduce a brand-new author to American Romance! Prepare yourself to be pulled in by Shelley Galloway's characters, who you'll just love. Cinderella Christmas *is a charming tale of a woman whose need for a particular pair of shoes starts a chain of events worthy not only of a Cinderella story, but of a fairy tale touched with the magic of Christmas.*

Oh, the shoes were on sale now. The beautiful shoes with the three gold·straps, the four-inch heel and not much else. The shoes that would show off a professional pedicure and the fine arch of her foot, and would set off an ivory lace gown to perfection.

Of course, to pull off an outfit like that, she would need to have the right kind of jewelry, Brooke Anne thought as she stared at the display through the high-class shop window. Nothing too bold…perhaps a simple diamond tennis bracelet and one-carat studs? Yes, that would lend an air of sophistication. Not too dramatic, but enough to let the outfit speak for itself. Elegance. Refinement. Money.

Hmm. And an elaborate updo for her hair. Something extravagant, to set off her gray eyes and high cheekbones. Something to give herself the illusion of height she so desperately needed. It was hard to look statuesque when you were five-foot-two.

But none of that would matter when she stepped out on the dance floor. Her date would hold her tightly and twirl her around and around. She would balance on the pad of her foot as they maneuvered carefully around the floor. She would put all those dancing lessons to good use, and her date would be impressed that she could waltz with ease. They would glide through the motions, twirling, dipping, stepping together. Other dancers would stay out of their way.

No, no one would be in the way…they would have already moved aside to watch the incredible display of footwork, the vision of two bodies in perfect harmony, moving in step, gliding in precise motion. They would stare at the striking woman, wearing the most beautiful, decadent shoes…shoes that would probably only last one evening, they were so fragile.

She would look like a modern-day Mona Lisa—with blond hair and gray eyes, though. And short. She would be a short Mona Lisa. But, still graceful.

But that wouldn't matter, because she would have on the most spectacular shoes that she'd ever seen. She'd feel like…*magic.*

"May I help you?"

Brooke Anne simply stared at the slim, elegant salesman who appeared beside her. "Pardon?"

He pursed his lips, then spoke again. "Miss, do you need any help? I noticed that you've been looking in the window for a few minutes."

"No…thanks."

With a twinge of humor, Brooke Anne glanced in the window again, this time to catch the reflection staring back at her. Here she was, devoid of makeup, her hair pulled back in a hurried ponytail, dressed in old jeans and a sweatshirt that was emblazoned with Jovial Janitor Service. And her shoes…she was wearing old tennis shoes.

Pamela Browning has eaten breakfast with Santa. It was a pancake breakfast fund-raiser for charity, exactly like the one in her book, and she attended dressed as Big Bird. She thought she'd be able to relax with a big plate of pancakes after leading the kids in songs from "Sesame Street," but some of the more thoughtful children had prepared her a plate of—you guessed it—birdseed. When she's not dressing as an eight-foot-tall bird, Pam spends her time canoeing, taking Latin-dance lessons and, lately, rebuilding her hurricane-damaged house.

Bah, humbug!

The Santa suit was too short.

Tom Collyer stared in dismay at his wrists, protruding from the fur-trimmed red plush sleeves. He'd get Leanne for this someday. There was a limit to how much a big brother should do for a sister.

The pancake breakfast was the Bigbee County, Texas, event of the year for little kids, and when Leanne had asked him to participate in this year's fund-raiser for the Homemakers' Club, he hadn't taken her seriously. He was newly home from his stint in the Marine Corps, and he hadn't yet adjusted his thinking back to Texas Hill Country standards. But his brother-in-law, Leanne's husband, had come down with an untimely case of the flu, and Tom had been roped into the Santa gig.

He peered out of the closet at the one hundred kids running around the Farish Township volunteer fire department headquarters, which was where they held these blamed breakfasts every year. One of the boys was hammering another boy's head against the floor, and his mother was trying to pry them apart. A little girl with long auburn curls stood wailing in a corner.

Leanne jumped onto a low bench and clapped her hands. "Children, guess what? It's time to tell Santa Claus what you want for Christmas! Have you all been good this year?"

"Yes!" the kids shouted, except for one boy in a blue velvet suit, who screamed, "No!" A nearby Santa's helper tried to shush him, but he merely screamed "No!" again. Tom did a double take. The helper, who resembled the boy so closely that she must be his mother, had long gleaming wheat-blond hair. It swung over her cheeks when she bent to talk to the child. Tom let his gaze travel downward, and took in the high firm breasts under a clinging white sweater, the narrow waist and gently rounded hips. He was craning his neck for a better assessment of those attributes when a loud-speaker began playing "Jingle Bells." That was his cue.

After pulling his pants down to cover his ankles and plumping his pillow-enhanced stomach to better hide his rangy frame, he drew a deep breath and strode from the closet.

"Ho-ho-ho!" he said, making his deep voice even deeper. "Merry Christmas!" As directed, he headed for the elaborate throne on the platform at one end of the room.

"Santa, Santa," cried several kids.

"Okay, boys and girls, remember that you're supposed to sit at the tables and eat your breakfast," Leanne instructed. "Santa's helper elves will come to each table in turn to take you to Santa Claus. Remember to smile! An elf will take your picture when you're sitting on Santa's knee."

Tom brushed away a strand of fluffy white wig hair that was tickling his face. "Ho-ho-ho!" he boomed again in his deep faux-Santa Claus voice as he eased his unaccustomed bulk down on the throne and ceremoniously drew the first kid onto his lap. "What do you want for Christmas, little girl?"

"A brand-new candy-red PT Cruiser with a convertible top and a turbo-charged engine," she said demurely.

"A car! Isn't that wonderful! Ho-ho-ho!" he said, sliding the kid off his lap as soon as the male helper elf behind the tripod snapped a picture. Was he supposed to promise delivery of such extravagant requests? Tom had no idea.

For the next fifteen minutes or so, Tom listened as kids asked for Yu-Gi-Oh! cards, Bratz dolls, even a Learjet. He was wondering what on earth a Crash Team Bandicoot was when he started counting the minutes; only an hour or so, and he'd be out of there. "Ho-ho-ho!" he said again and again. "Merry Christmas!"

Out of the corners of his eyes, Tom spotted the kid in the blue velvet suit approaching. He scanned the crowd for the boy's gorgeous mother, who was temporarily distracted by a bottle of spilled syrup at one of the tables.

"Ho-ho-ho!" Tom chortled as a helper elf nudged the kid in the blue suit toward him. And when the kid hurled a heretofore concealed cup of orange juice into his lap, Tom's chortle became "Ho-ho-ho—oh, no!" The kid stood there, frowning. Tom shot him a dirty look and, using the handkerchief that he'd had the presence of mind to stuff into his pocket, swiped hastily at the orange rivulets gathering in his crotch. With great effort, he managed to bite back a four-letter word that drill sergeants liked to say when things weren't going well.

He jammed the handkerchief back in his pocket and hoisted the boy onto his knee. "Careful now," Tom said. "Mustn't get orange juice on that nice blue suit, ho-ho-ho!"

"Do you always laugh like that?" asked the kid, who seemed about five years old. He had a voice like a foghorn and a scowl that would do justice to Scrooge himself.

"Laugh like what?" Tom asked, realizing too late that he'd used his own voice, not Santa's.

"'Ho-ho-ho.' Nobody laughs like that." The boy was regarding him with wide blue eyes.

"Ho-ho-ho," Tom said, lapsing back into his Santa voice. "You're a funny guy, right?"

"No, I'm not. You aren't, either."

"Ahem," Santa said. "Maybe you should just tell me what you want for Christmas."

The kid glowered at him. "Guess," he said.

Tom was unprepared for this. "An Etch-a-Sketch?" he ventured. Those had been popular when he was a child.

"Nope."

"Yu-Gi-Oh! cards? A Crash Team Billy Goat…uh, I mean Bandicoot?"

"Nope."

Beads of sweat broke out on Tom's forehead. The helpers were unaware of his plight. They were busy lining up the other kids who wanted to talk to Santa.

"Yu-Gi-Oh! cards?"

"You already guessed that one." The boy's voice was full of scorn.

"A bike? Play-Doh?"

The kid jumped off his lap, disconcerting the elf with the camera. "I want a real daddy for Christmas," the boy said, and stared defiantly up at Tom....

*This is Mary Anne Wilson's third book in her
four-book miniseries entitled*
RETURN TO SILVER CREEK,
*the dramatic stories of four men who became fast
friends as youths in a small Nevada town—and the
unexpected turns each of their lives has taken.
Cane Stone's tale is no exception!*

A month ago, Las Vegas, Nevada

"I'm not going back to Silver Creek," Cane Stone said. "I don't have the time, or the inclination to make the time. Besides, it's not home for me."

The man he was talking to, Jack Prescott, shook his head, then motioned with both hands at Cane's penthouse. It was done in black and white—black marble floors, white stone fireplace, white leather furniture. The only splash of color came from the sofa pillows, in various shades of red. "This is home?"

The Dream Catcher Hotel and Casino on The Strip in Las Vegas was a place to be. The place Cane worked. The part of the world that he owned. But a home? No. He'd never had one. "It's my place," he said honestly.

An angular man, dressed as usual in faded jeans, an old open-necked shirt and well-worn leather boots—despite the millions he was worth—Jack leaned back against the semi-circular couch, positioned to face the bank of windows that looked down on the sprawling city twenty stories below. "Cane, come on. You haven't been back for years, and it's the holidays."

"Bah, humbug," Cane said with a slight smile, wishing that the feeble joke would ease the growing tension in him. A tension that had started when Jack had asked him to go back to Silver Creek. "You know that for people like us there are no holidays. They're the heavy times in the year. I look forward to Christmas the way Ebenezer Scrooge did. You get through it and make as much money as you can."

Jack didn't respond with any semblance of a smile. Instead, he muttered, "God, you're cynical."

"Realistic," Cane amended with a shrug. "What I want to know, though, is why it's so important to you that I go to Silver Creek?"

"I said, it's the holidays, and that means friends. Josh is there now, and Gordie, who's in his clinic twenty-four hours a day. We can get drunk, ski down Main Street, take on Killer Run again. Whatever you want."

Jack, Josh and Gordie were as close to a family as Cane had come as a child. The orphanage hadn't been anything out of Dickens, but it hadn't been family. The three friends were. The four of them had done everything together, including getting into trouble and wiping out on Killer Run. "Tempting," Cane said, a pure lie at that moment. "But no deal."

"I won't stop asking," Jack said.

Cane stood and crossed to the built-in bar by the bank of windows. He ignored the alcohol and glasses and picked up one of several packs of unopened cards, catching a glimpse of himself in the mirrors behind the bar before he turned to Jack. He was tall, about Jack's height at six-foot-one or so, with dark hair worn a bit long like Jack's, and brushed by gray—like Jack's. His eyes, though, were deep blue, in contrast to Jack's, which were almost black.

He was sure he could match Jack dollar for dollar if he had to. And where just as Jack didn't look like the richest man in Silver Creek, Cane didn't look like a wealthy hotel/casino owner in Las Vegas. Few owners dressed in Levi's and T-shirts; even fewer went without any jewelry, including a watch. He had a closetful of expensive suits and silk shirts, but he hardly ever wore them. Still, he fit right in at the Dream Catcher Hotel and Casino. It was about the only place he'd ever felt he fit in. He didn't fit in Silver Creek. He never had.

He went back to Jack with the cards, broke the seal on the deck and said as he slipped the cards out of the package, "Let's settle this once and for all."

"I'm not going to play poker with you," Jack told him. "I don't stand a chance."

Cane eyed his friend as he sat down by him on the couch. "We'll keep it simple," he murmured. He took the cards out of the box, tossed the empty box on the onyx coffee table in front of them and shuffled the deck.

"What's at stake?" Jack asked.

"If you win, I'll head north to Silver Creek for a few days around the holidays…"

HARLEQUIN®

AMERICAN *Romance*®

This season, enjoy a holiday fairy tale by a
brand-new author…

CINDERELLA CHRISTMAS

by Shelley Galloway

(November 2005)

When she's wearing her mop-emblazoned
Jovial Janitor uniform, most people look
right through Brooke Anne Kessler. But
Royal Hotels executive Morgan Carmichael
has just been jilted by his date for the
company Christmas ball, and suddenly
he's seeing the petite blonde who dusts his
office in a whole different light.…

Available wherever Harlequin books are sold.

If you enjoyed what you just read,
then we've got an offer you can't resist!

Take 2 bestselling
love stories FREE!
Plus get a FREE surprise gift!

Clip this page and mail it to Harlequin Reader Service®

IN U.S.A.	IN CANADA
3010 Walden Ave.	P.O. Box 609
P.O. Box 1867	Fort Erie, Ontario
Buffalo, N.Y. 14240-1867	L2A 5X3

YES! Please send me 2 free Harlequin American Romance® novels and my free surprise gift. After receiving them, if I don't wish to receive anymore, I can return the shipping statement marked cancel. If I don't cancel, I will receive 4 brand-new novels every month, before they're available in stores! In the U.S.A., bill me at the bargain price of $4.24 plus 25¢ shipping & handling per book and applicable sales tax, if any*. In Canada, bill me at the bargain price of $4.99 plus 25¢ shipping & handling per book and applicable taxes**. That's the complete price and a savings of at least 10% off the cover prices—what a great deal! I understand that accepting the 2 free books and gift places me under no obligation ever to buy any books. I can always return a shipment and cancel at any time. Even if I never buy another book from Harlequin, the 2 free books and gift are mine to keep forever.

154 HDN DZ7S
354 HDN DZ7T

Name	(PLEASE PRINT)	
Address	Apt.#	
City	State/Prov.	Zip/Postal Code

Not valid to current Harlequin American Romance® subscribers.

Want to try two free books from another series?
Call 1-800-873-8635 or visit www.morefreebooks.com.

* Terms and prices subject to change without notice. Sales tax applicable in N.Y.
** Canadian residents will be charged applicable provincial taxes and GST.
  All orders subject to approval. Offer limited to one per household.
  ® are registered trademarks owned and used by the trademark owner and or its licensee.

AMER04R   ©2004 Harlequin Enterprises Limited

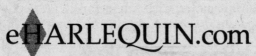

eHARLEQUIN.com

The Ultimate Destination for Women's Fiction

For **FREE online reading,** visit
www.eHarlequin.com now and enjoy:

Online Reads
Read **Daily** and **Weekly** chapters from
our Internet-exclusive stories by your
favorite authors.

Interactive Novels
Cast your vote to help decide how these
stories unfold...then stay tuned!

Quick Reads
For shorter romantic reads, try our
collection of Poems, Toasts, & More!

Online Read Library
Miss one of our online reads?
Come here to catch up!

Reading Groups
Discuss, share and rave with other
community members!

For great reading online,
visit www.eHarlequin.com today!

INTONL04R

AMERICAN *Romance*®

Presenting…

CHRISTMAS, TEXAS STYLE

A holiday gift for readers of
Harlequin American Romance

Novellas from three of
your favorite authors

Four Texas Babies
TINA LEONARD

A Texan Under the Mistletoe
LEAH VALE

Merry Texmas
LINDA WARREN

*Available November 2005 wherever
Harlequin books are sold.*

HARCTS1105

AMERICAN *Romance*®

COMING NEXT MONTH

#1089 CHRISTMAS, TEXAS STYLE by Tina Leonard, Leah Vale and Linda Warren

What makes a Christmas spent in Texas so special? Find out in three heartwarming stories about family, romance and the true meaning of the holidays, by three of your favorite Harlequin American Romance authors.

#1090 CINDERELLA CHRISTMAS by Shelley Galloway

When she's wearing her mop-emblazoned Jovial Janitor uniform, Brooke Anne Kessler finds that most people look right through her. But Royal Hotels executive Morgan Carmichael has just been jilted by his date for the company Christmas ball, and suddenly he's seeing the petite blonde who dusts his office in a whole different light....

#1091 BREAKFAST WITH SANTA by Pamela Browning

Fatherhood

When Tom Collyer unwillingly subs as Santa Claus for the annual Farish, Texas, Breakfast with Santa pancake fest, the last thing he expects is the request he gets from one five-year-old boy. Or how he and the little boy's breathtakingly beautiful mother will end up satisfying it!

#1092 HOLIDAY HOMECOMING by Mary Anne Wilson

Return to Silver Creek

Cane Stone is back in a town he couldn't wait to get away from—but only because he took a chance on a bet and lost. Holly Winston isn't too happy he's back, either. She can never forgive him for the breakup of her marriage. The odds are against these two having a relationship. But sometimes you *can* beat the odds.